Billy

Billy

Laura Roybal

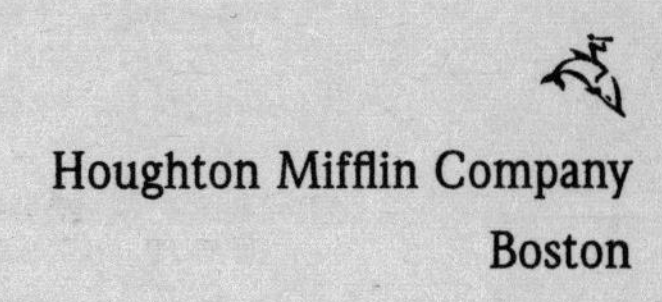

Houghton Mifflin Company
Boston

Library of Congress Cataloging-in-Publication Data

Roybal, Laura.
Billy/ by Laura Roybal. p. cm.
Summary: Billy, a sixteen-year-old boy who becomes reunited with the family he was kidnapped from by his natural father six years earlier, tries to sort out his identity.
RNF ISBN 0-395-67649-5 PAP ISBN 0-395-96062-2
[1. Identity — Fiction. 2. Fathers and sons — Fiction.
3. Kidnapping — Fiction.] I. Title.
PZ7.R81595Bi 1994
[Fic] — dc20 93-4837 CIP AC

Printed in the United States of America
OPM 10 9 8 7 6 5 4 3 2 1

To Jamie and Amanda and to Juanita Roybal
who always made me feel at home

ONE

The Barrel Cactus served a good lunch, but technically it was a bar and I wasn't supposed to be there, especially at one-thirty in the afternoon on a regular school day. But when the village marshal walked in he barely gave me a glance.

Charlie Silva had been marshal since something just short of forever. He was probably seventy by now, but he was lean, compact, and tough as a man half his age, and his hair and mustache were still black, with just the faintest sprinkling of silver. But Charlie was still The Law, in capital letters, and I suddenly wished I had decided to wait around the gas station for the bus instead of coming in here, that I had a glass of ginger ale sitting on the corner of the pool table instead of a beer, that I wasn't in trouble with the principal.... Basically, I wished all the things you would wish when you're suddenly face-to-face with The Law.

But Charlie didn't say anything, which is maybe one of the reasons he's still alive after more than thirty years as marshal. He sat down at the counter and ordered a plate of tamales and a cup of coffee, then turned around on the stool and studied not me, but the pool table.

"Never make that shot," he commented.

I didn't, either. Maybe I could have if he hadn't been there staring at me. I'm not a bad player, normally. Then again, maybe not. I rolled the last two balls in by hand and racked up the cue.

"School out early?" Charlie asked.

He knew it wasn't. You can always tell when school's out by the hordes of kids roaming around town. I was the only one between four and nineteen on the loose.

"It is for me. Out early today, and three more days off."

"Fighting," he said. In Spanish, though. *"Peleando."*

"I didn't start anything," I said.

"You never do. But you are pretty quick to finish it, *qué no?"*

"Am I? Or am I just the one who gets the blame whenever something happens?"

"You're not the whining type."

I pulled up a stool next to him and sat down, leaning backwards on the bar. I left the beer sitting on the corner of the pool table, hoping maybe he'd think someone before me had left it there. Of course, there's another reason why he's been marshal for so long. He's not particularly stupid, either.

"Okay. So I'm guilty. But I was brought up to believe that decent men should defend women who are being picked on."

"Me, too. So, who were you fighting with?"

His dinner came, and he swung around in his seat to eat.

"Joe Gallegos."

It was not the first time Joe and me had come down to blows. Joe rubbed me the wrong way, usually on purpose. He was taller than me by several inches, but skinny. A greasy, long-haired kid who thought he was some big city gang leader or something. I lived up the canyon, almost twenty miles out from town. My dad was an ex-rodeo man, and most of my best friends ran cattle in the wilderness. I guess we all dressed and acted like cowboys. In fact, half the school called Cody Walken, Bobby Hernandez, Cip Delgado, and me the Canyon Cowboys. All this irritated Joe Gallegos because having guys like us in the school just rubbed it in that he was a hick, same as the rest of us.

"Joe was picking on Dana?" Charlie asked, wiping chile off his mustache.

I was surprised how much he knew about my love life, but I said, "No. Rosemary Rivera."

"Since when did you take up with her?"

"Since never, and I never will, either. But when a girl is slapping on a guy and hollering for him to leave her alone, I tend to figure she might need some assistance."

"So, you hit him."

"Not right away. But, yeah. I hit him."

"And you got suspended."

"Yeah."

"Did Joe get suspended?"

"No. But then, the one that's bleeding the most tends to get the most sympathy."

"I suppose Rosemary thinks you're a knight in shining armor now."

"Uh. No. Rosemary slapped me for hitting Joe and threatened my life if I ever do it again."

"Oh. Does Dana think you're a big, strong hero for rescuing a damsel in distress?"

"Dana thinks I'm going with Rosemary now, and she won't talk to me."

"You won the fight, Coyote, but it looks like that's about all you did right."

I stared down at the knuckles of my right hand where they were bruised and torn, and felt stupid. Fighting never made me feel like a hero anyway, but Charlie's quiet little chat made me wish I was about a thousand miles away. He just sat there, working his way through his lunch, letting me feel like a fool. Like I said, there's a good reason why he's been marshal so long.

"You like to fight, Coyote?" he asked finally.

"Not really."

"Seems like you're always getting into trouble at school for fighting. You must like it. Or maybe your daddy just raised you too rough."

"You can't blame my dad," I said. "I've only known him five years. It's just that Gallegos. Every time I see him I want to wipe his face on the parking lot."

"Me, too," Charlie said. "A lot of people affect me that way. But if I hit them just because of who they are, what would that make me?"

"Not marshal anyway."

"Nada. Nothing. Just like they are." He wiped up the last bit of chile off his plate with his tortilla and ate it while I thought that over. *"Oye,* Coyote. You need a ride home? I have to go up that way, check on my horses."

"Yeah. Thanks."

He paid for his lunch and picked up his hat. I followed him to the marshal's car that was parked out front and we climbed in and headed north up the canyon. He was the village marshal and he had a house in town, but Charlie was from an old ranching family and still owned a chunk of land up the canyon, not too far from where Dad and me lived.

"Charlie," I said. "What would you do if . . . I mean, suppose there was this girl that . . . well, you almost felt like you didn't want to live without her, but she was mad at you. She said she would never talk to you again and wouldn't listen to anything you said. What would you do?"

"Well." Charlie considered, stroking his mustache thoughtfully with a knuckle. "If I had a problem like that, I think maybe what I'd do is go on up to the dance at the Mountain View Bar on Friday night, where that girl would likely be. I'd go up with my friends, and I'd have a few Cokes to drink, if I was under age, like you. But I might just *pretend* to be a little high, and I might say something real loud, near where the girl and all her friends could hear, about how much I missed her, and how she misunderstood everything, and how I'd hate to live without her. If I had that sort of problem, I might just try something like that."

"Oh, yeah, right," I said, laughing. But I was thinking, really, it wasn't such a bad idea.

Dad and I lived in a two-story log cabin about eight miles up from where the two-lane paved highway faded into a lane-and-a-half clay-and-gravel road. The cabin was on the west side of the road, with Sal's Bar straight across the street on the east, though the mountain was so steep there that Sal's front steps were about level with our roof. It was a nice place to live. The narrow dirt road was almost free of traffic except when the tourists trundled by in their Winnebagos in the summer, and the nearest neighbor, except Sal, was miles off, all the land around us belonging to the Forest Service.

Charlie let me off on the road just above the house instead of going down the driveway. I waved goodbye and walked down and around to the door, trying not to get knocked over by Rex, who, as usual, was bounding all over me and slobbering. I played with him a little, then went inside to light the fires and pull a packet of elk meat out of the freezer for dinner. In that narrow, dark canyon, the cabin was a cold place when it was empty all day, but a fire in the wood stove in the kitchen and another one crackling in the fireplace made it warm and cheerful in just a few minutes. I took care of all the usual chores, like bringing in firewood, carrying out ashes, peeling potatoes. Then I sat down at the table to do my homework. I didn't really mind a three-day suspension from school, but I was glad Dad was working in town. That meant it would be hours yet before I had to tell him about it.

TWO

Friday evening Dad and Sal Delgado watched me practice roping in Sal's corral below the bar. Sal lounged on the fence, just watching, but Dad sat on the top rail timing me with a stopwatch.

"Nine and three," he said looking up. "That won't take you to the pros."

"It's not bad time," Sal said. "Consistency is more important than speed. You lose a calf in the second or third round and a record time in the first means nothing."

Dad studied the stopped clock in his hand. "Do it again," he said.

I didn't mind doing it again. Practice was what I was out there for in the first place. I got my ropes ready and put San Pablo and the calf back into the chutes Dad had rigged up. Calf roping is an interesting sport, because you not only need eye-hand coordination and a good sense of timing and distance for catching the calf with the rope, you also have to be able to throw it and tie up its feet—without knots—so that it can't get up and walk off. This time, fifth try of the night, I did my best time, but the calf got up and struggled out of the rope, sick of playing this game, before the time limit on his staying on the ground was up.

"You need a new horse," Dad said suddenly as I picked up my ropes.

"He needs his own calf," Sal grumbled. "He's running all the weight off mine, and I have to sell them to make a living."

"San Pablo's a good horse, but he's not a roping horse," Dad said, ignoring Sal. "He makes you work too hard. A good horse wouldn't have let that calf get up either."

"Dad," I said, "are you thinking about buying a real roping horse?"

Dad tapped the knob on the watch so it would go back to zero. "I don't know, Son," he said finally. "A horse like that wouldn't come for less than a thousand dollars, and we don't exactly have money to throw away. Just how serious are you about this rodeo business anyway?"

"Serious," I said.

Dad looked over at Sal.

"You want to know if you can keep a horse in my corral? You feed it, that's all I have to say. You don't buy feed, it don't eat. And while you're at it, buy yourself a cow, too. Raise your own beef for chasing."

Dad looked back over at me. "I'm not making any promises," he said sharply. "But...I guess I could keep my eyes open for a good deal."

"Thanks, Dad," I said.

He jumped down from the corral rail and slid the stopwatch into his pocket. "Hang it up for tonight. I got to go get ready for the dance."

"Yeah. Me, too. I'll be in after I put everything away here."

He nodded without answering, and walked back to the house. Sal turned to climb up to the road and cross back to his bar. I unsaddled San Pablo, rubbed him down, and gave him a can full of grain to go with his dinner. The tack all went into a little shed next to the back porch. Ropes, chaps, and spurs went into the house with me to be put away properly. I learned a long time back that if I wanted to do things like ride horses, I had to take care of all the gear involved. Dad didn't mind dirty dishes left lying around, but he'd kick my butt if I ever went in and left a saddle or a lasso where it didn't belong.

The shower was running when I went in. I went upstairs and put away my gear. When I heard the water turn off, I took a towel and went back down, going into the bathroom as Dad came out.

The cabin was two floors, but it was only two rooms, too. Downstairs was a combined kitchen and living room. Upstairs, the stairwell split two sides of one big bedroom. The bathroom was fitted into all this as an afterthought, obviously. It occupied the space under the stairs.

I had already decided what I was going to wear to the dance: my best jeans and boots, a brand-new roper shirt, my good Stetson. It was just another dance at the local bar, but I knew Dana was going to be there and I wanted to be sure she knew I was there, too. She hadn't talked to me all week, and I was thinking seriously of giving Charlie's plan a try.

Dad, I could tell, was planning to impress some female, too. When I came back up, he was already wearing his least-faded jeans and fanciest cowboy shirt. He was polishing his boots, and had stuck one of his biggest, gaudiest buckles on his belt. Some rodeos give out belt buckles instead of prize money, and Dad had a fair collection of them. He usually kept them all in a shoebox on the closet shelf, but if he was trying to look impressive he pulled out the box and rifled through it to find something fancy.

"You got a date, or you hoping to get lucky?" I asked him, teasing.

I was kind of surprised when he didn't answer right off. He looked up at me from under an eyebrow and said finally, "I'm taking Linda Lucero."

"Are you crazy? She's married!"

"Her and Justanano been split up for months," he

said, looking back down at the boot he was polishing.

"You mean she's been going out on him for months. They aren't really divorced or anything yet. Dad, he carries a gun!"

"I know."

He put down the brush and pulled his boots on, but he still sat there inspecting his boot toes while I dressed. "I've known Linda since we were kids," he said finally.

"Yeah, but I know you. You don't get out those belt buckles for childhood buddies."

"She's a good dancer."

"And good-looking."

"Uh-huh. Just a minute, here. I'm a little confused. Isn't it the parent who checks on the child's dates and gives advice?"

"I guess it all depends. Dad . . ."

"Yeah?"

"Just be careful, huh?"

"I'm not stupid, Billy," he said. "You, on the other hand . . ."

"Ah, Dad, come on!"

"You watch yourself," he said seriously.

"Dad, I can handle myself just fine. I'm more worried about you."

"I'm not the one who just got suspended for half a week for fighting. Don't they have dances at school anymore?"

"Not many. Why?"

"I don't like you going to the bars the way you do. All you kids, I mean, not just you. When I was your age, they had dances or roller skating or something over at the VFW hall every weekend. Now, there's nothing for kids to do in town but go to the bars."

"Maybe because someone burned the VFW hall down ten years ago."

"Or maybe because people spend more time bitching about how wild kids are than they spend giving those kids something safe to do. Are you going with Dana?"

"Uh. No. I'm going with Cody and the guys."

"Well, you stay out of trouble. "I'll be there, remember. I catch you drinking *y te pataleo.*"

"Yes, sir," I said.

"I'm serious, Billy. You're in enough trouble as it is. You want to be treated like an adult, but that means being responsible like an adult and following the rules like an adult would."

"Yes, sir," I said again, but more serious this time. He looked at me for a moment, sharp and level, then he nodded, satisfied that I wasn't bullshitting him.

"See you at the dance, then. And by the way, make sure your truck has gas. We're going for wood tomorrow. Be ready to go by six-thirty, sharp."

He left then. A few seconds later I heard his old car

choke into life, and the tires spinning on the loose dirt as he drove up the steep driveway. It was typical of him not to set me some specific time to be home, but to drop a warning like that in my lap before I left. If we were leaving to go cut firewood at six-thirty in the morning (and he meant that; he wouldn't be late himself), that meant I had to be up by five-thirty to get dressed and eat and get the truck ready to go. It also meant that we'd spend the entire day chopping down trees, trimming them, cutting them up, loading them into the truck, unloading them at home, and going back for more. Dad figured I was old enough to know how much sleep I needed for a day like that, and if I didn't get in at a decent time, the suffering I'd do the next day would be better punishment than anything he could think up.

As I finished dressing, I considered Dad and the few girls he'd dated in the past five years. I guessed I was really pretty lucky. I knew that better than half the kids at school either had a single-parent family or were living with stepparents, so I heard a lot about other kids' problems with their mom's boyfriends or their dad's girlfriends. For one thing, being a boy living with my dad made life simpler. Everyone wants to mother a girl living with a dad, and when a guy is living with only a mother, all her boyfriends seem to think they have to be pals with the kid. Dad dated, but he kept things simple for both of us by never asking anyone to move in with us (be hard to anyway, with only one bedroom). I know kids that are half crazy from their parent's girlfriends or boyfriends trying to raise them.

I wasn't too pleased that this time he'd picked a still-married woman to take to the dance, but I suppose if Dad didn't take her, someone else would. She was pretty, and she could dance good, and except for treating her husband like dirt, she wasn't too bad. Girls in Monte Verde tended early toward marriage or relationships, and there weren't a lot of single ones Dad's age for him to choose from. I was thinking, as I grabbed my hat and ran out to meet Cody on the road, that Dad probably would be out pretty late himself tonight.

"We can use my dad's camp only if we go on the last hunt," Cipi said. His dad was Sal Delgado.

"The Circle J has a secondary camp we can use anytime we want," Cody said. "It's way up in the Wilderness, past Round Mountain and toward the peaks."

"Nice," Cip said. "But Billy and me can't go on any hunt. We promised Dad to guide and wrangle horses on the first two to pay for the horses we plan to use for the third."

"So, if we're going up alone, it has to be the third hunt," Cody said, looking disgusted.

"If we were going to Spring Mountain it would be worthless, but we got a choice of two wilderness camps," Cip said. "The deer'll run like crazy off Spring Mountain after the first day of the hunt, and where can they go but up?"

"You hope."

"Well, what else are they gonna do? Hide out in the Barrel Cactus? Don't be so picky, man. Some of us have to work for a living, right, Billy?"

Dana was wearing her new boots. The jeans she had tucked into them were so tight they looked painted on. Her hair was a cloud of black curls, held out of her face by a silver barrette...

"Hey, Coyote!"

"Huh? What?"

"We're talking about the hunting trip, man."

"Yeah. Well, I can only go on the last hunt. I promised to wrangle horses the first two to pay Sal for the rent of San Pablo."

"Yeah," Bobby said, grinning at me. "We heard."

"You still mooning around over that chick?" Cody said. "Either go get her, or forget her, man."

"Yeah. I will," I said. She was wearing the earrings I gave her, half a dozen silver stars hanging from silver chains. They flashed and glittered in the colored lights behind the band.

"We're never going to get this together," Cody said.

"Look, what's the problem anyway?" Bobby said. "The last hunt's the longest, and they don't even start till November anyway. We'll have all the details worked out by then. Meantime . . ."

"Yes?" Cody said.

"I'm going to ask Julie Rios to dance." He adjusted the angle of his cowboy hat and headed off through the crowd.

"We do still have plenty of time for details," Cip said. I mean, what's to arrange, anyway? We sight in our rifles anytime between now and the hunt, go shopping for food the day before. Big deal."

"Big enough," Cody said. "The last hunt has three school days in it. Your dad going to let you off school? I bet you haven't even asked."

"If I stay out of trouble in school from now on, I can have the three days off," I said.

Her shirt was low-cut and tight and a lot of dark coffee-and-cream colored skin showed above it. There was another glimmer of silver at her throat.

"Huh," Cody said. "Your dad lets you get away with murder."

"Dad said he doesn't like to take hunting away as a punishment. Long as I don't get suspended again, trip's still on."

"Cip won't get any school time off," Cody said.

"I got the same three days, same rules," Cip said.

"I'm astounded," Cody said. "You two are prepared."

"I'm not missing this hunt for anything," Cip said. "And I'm not gonna do anything to screw it up either. *Digame, amigo,* is your dad gonna let you take off school to wander through the wilderness alone with a loaded rifle?"

"*I* was figuring on the first hunt, the weekend," Cody said.

"Figure again," Cip said.

Dad stepped up to the bar then.

"Billy."

"Oh. Hi, Dad."

He gave only a brief nod to Cody and Cipi and said, "I'm leaving."

"Yeah. I figured. I just saw Justo come in."

"Uh-huh," Dad said. "He's already drunk and looking for an excuse to punch somebody. And he's got two cousins and a brother with him."

"Yeah. I noticed."

Dad laid a hand on my shoulder. "Billy, you stay out of trouble tonight."

"Sure, Dad."

"Billy," Dad said sharply in his pay-attention voice. I looked at him. Paid attention.

"You are sixteen years old—barely—in a bar in a twenty-one state, with beer-breath I could smell halfway across the room and a moony look in your eyes over a girl who's dancing with someone else. That sounds like a good recipe for trouble to me. You start a fight at school, you get a reputation as a troublemaker with the principal. But you start something here, and the state cops will finish it for you. You ever think about that?"

"Uh, no," I said. "I didn't."

"Do it."

"Yeah. I am."

He gave my shoulder a squeeze and dropped his hand. "Good. By the way, when you get home tonight, I'm gonna kick your butt for drinking. I warned you."

"Yeah. You did."

He grinned at me and ducked back into the crowd. A second later, he was escorting Linda Lucero out the front door. I watched him, thinking about state cops, like he said, and wondering how serious this thing with Linda was going to turn out to be, but it all went out of my head the next second as Dana and one of her friends moved in closer to the bar. Time for Charlie's plan.

"Cody," I said, shouting louder than I had to over the music, "Cody, I don't know what I'm going to do."

"Yeah," Cody said, giving me a peculiar look. I hadn't mentioned The Plan to him. "Beats me, too."

"I just don't know, Cody. I don't think that busting Joe Gallegos for any reason—*any reason*—is a mistake. Do you?"

"Uh. No."

"Well, Dana thinks so!" I increased the volume, just in case she wasn't listening. "She won't even talk to me. Just because I found some dumb reason to hit him... I don't even remember what the reason was, but she won't talk to me."

"So what?" Cody asked. He still wasn't sure what was going on. He was leaning back on his boot heels to distance himself a little from my shouting.

"I can't stand it when she won't talk to me!" I yelled at him. "I love her, Cody, I don't want to live without her! What should I do?"

"Why don't you shut up?" Dana hissed in my ear. "You're making a spectacle of yourself."

"I don't care, and I'm going to keep it up until you talk to me. Please, Dana, just talk to me."

She sighed and rolled her eyes, like this whole thing was too disgusting for words. The girl with her giggled.

"All right. I'll talk. What do you want me to say?"

"Outside.

"What?"

"Talk to me outside. Just for a minute."

"Oh, all right!"

It was quieter outside, with the blare of the band muffled by the thick adobe walls of the building. It was cool, too. The breeze came right down from the high country and it had the taste of winter in it. A lot of people were in the parking lot getting out of the noise and stuffiness of the dance. Dana and I didn't stay in the parking lot, though; we walked around to the back side of the bar, where there was a narrow strip of ground before a cliff dropped off fifty feet straight down to the river. Back there it was even quieter; you could hear the rush of the water under the noise of the dance. It was darker, too. There was no moon, just a million stars in a cold, black sky.

"Don't touch me," Dana said.

I did anyway. I caught her arm to keep her from running away from me, then I got both arms around her and just pulled her close. Somehow, that seemed like a better idea than trying to talk it out anyway. She stiffened against me at first, but then she relaxed into my embrace.

"Let's not fight anymore," I said.

She didn't answer, but she didn't stomp on my foot to make me let go, either. She'd done that once before and nearly crippled me. I kissed her cheek gently, the curve of her ear.

"I love you," I said.

She pushed against my shoulders and I released her,

but she didn't step away, she just wanted enough space to look me in the eye.

"Really?"

"Really," I said.

"And Rosemary was just an excuse to hit Joe Gallegos?"

"Honest. You know I'd never have anything to do with her."

"You mean she'd never have anything to do with you."

"Dana..."

"You look harder for an excuse next time," she said, sliding back into my arms.

It was like a weight lifting. I opened my mouth to breathe and my chest felt lighter, the air came in easier than it had in days. I kissed her again. Then we just stood there on the cliff, with my arms around her and her head tucked up against my chest. She shivered.

"We better go back in," I said.

"Yeah. Okay."

"Can I drive you home tonight?"

"You came with Cody."

"Oh. Yeah."

"Maybe tomorrow we can get together."

"No. I have to go with my dad to get wood."

She sighed. "Sunday?"

"I'll call you Sunday. I promise. Just dance with me

tonight," I said. "We'll work on the rest of it later."

"All right." I kissed her again and we walked, hand in hand, back to the parking lot. The minute we got around the building, she dropped my hand and ran to tell her friends that we'd made up. Cody, Cipi, and Bobby were leaning up against Cody's pickup, waiting for me.

"Got it all straightened out?" Cip asked, grinning.

"Yeah. I think so."

"Good," Bobby said. "You've been lousy company lately."

I laughed at that. The scent of Dana's perfume was still in my nose, and I felt almost high. When Joe Gallegos walked up, I hardly even recognized him.

"Was it any good?" he said.

I just stared at him. I had no idea what he was talking about.

"That little whore you took back there, is she any good? I've been thinking about buying some of that action myself. What's the charge?"

I didn't even think. I just went straight for his throat.

"You really did it this time," Charlie said.

It took about two seconds for a brawl to break out after I punched Joe Gallegos. There were a dozen state cops out there in a matter of minutes, and they busted at least fifty people. Mountain View Bar was ten miles from the village limits, way out of Charlie's jurisdiction. But he knew everyone involved in the brawl, and when he heard about it, he came down to the state police place in Santa Fe where they had us all to see what he could do.

I didn't have an answer for that, so I just sat there on the bench, staring at my hands. All the adults had been booked and released already, but there were about fifteen juveniles waiting to be picked up by their parents. Who would have thought punching Joe Gallegos would be the start of something this big?

Charlie walked over to the main desk to talk to the cop working there.

"Cody, I'm really sorry," I said.

"Why're you telling me?"

"'Cause you're eighteen. They could charge you like an adult for this. It could go on your permanent record and everything."

"Sixteen to twenty-one they can get you on adult charges after a hearing. We're all at least sixteen."

"Oh."

"Don't worry about it. That's just so they can lock up all these juvenile rapists and murderers for longer. They won't do that for a bar fight. They just dragged us all the way down here to scare us."

"It's working," Bobby said.

"Yeah," Cip and I agreed.

After a minute, Cody gave me a twisted grin and he said, "Yeah," too.

Mothers and fathers started showing up, singly and in small groups. Bobby's mom came for him. Joe Gallegos's dad came and cussed and carried on till the cops threatened to lock him up. Sal Delgado came for Cipi. Half an hour later, I was the only one left.

Charlie came back over with a Styrofoam cup of black coffee and sat down with me.

"Took a while to find your dad. He'll be here soon though."

I nodded. I was thinking that the worst thing about making a stupid mistake is that you can't take it back. Ever. "He was just telling me to stay out of trouble."

"But you didn't listen."

"I thought I did." I told him what Joe had said about Dana.

He shrugged, unimpressed. "I've heard worse. At least you're fighting over the right girl now. Does this mean the two of you made up?"

"Yeah, I think so. Maybe if I wasn't so wrapped up in thinking of her I wouldn't have started that fight, but I was. Sometimes I feel like I'm going crazy. I can't think of anything but Dana. Charlie, I think I want to marry her. But how can you tell if love like that is going to last a lifetime? And don't sit there and tell me I'm too young to feel that way, because I do."

"Oh, I don't doubt that, Coyote. You're never too young to love. All you're too young for is commitment. Marriage isn't a matter of passion and romance, it's a job. And with this job, you can't call in sick when you don't feel up to the challenge."

"But doesn't love . . . like . . . conquer the challenge?"

"No," he said, slurping at his coffee.

"It always does in the movies," I said.

"Life isn't a movie," he said.

"Well, no," I admitted.

"Marriage is a partnership. It's two people working together toward one common goal," Charlie said. Then he stopped and thought that over. "In fact, you could say marriage is a single unit, made up of two people. The marriage won't work without one hundred percent commitment from both people, and the people aren't whole without each other."

"Man. As if I didn't have enough to think about."

"It's a serious business, Coyote. Not something you do in a blind moment of passion, believe me. The important thing to remember is that it's okay to walk out on love, if the commitment isn't there to make a marriage work."

"Sounds almost like something Dad told me."

"Yeah. I figured that. He never married your mama, did he?"

"Well, no. But when they broke up, he didn't know about me, being on the way, I mean."

"Don't matter. A baby is one of the worst reasons there is for getting into a marriage. You have one goal, she has a different one, and the baby holds you both away from them. That's disaster in the making from day one."

"Huh."

I'd forgotten all about where I was and why. Charlie got up to refill his coffee cup, and I sat there on the bench considering what he'd said. I snapped back to reality, though, when Dad walked in. Thoughts of Dana crowded backwards. I looked around and saw again the bare walls, the barred windows, the uniforms. And Dad. He just stood there in the doorway looking at me. Reality greater than the law was my father, standing there, staring me down.

Dad moved finally. He took a step into the room and then stopped again as a patrolman came out of the back room with a long string of paper in his hand.

"Hey, Sarge, when we took those kids' prints, just to scare them, I ran them through the computer for something to do. And guess what? This one kid, Billy

Melendez, his prints match up with a William James Campbell who's been on a missing list for almost six years."

The desk sergeant snatched the paper to read it himself, then turned to stare at me. Charlie turned and gave me a slow, thoughtful look. The cop with the paper stared at me, too. Then, slowly, they all turned and looked at Dad. I thought, Holy shit.

THREE

The window faced east, and in the distance I could see the sun rising over the Sangre de Cristo Mountains. I'd been standing at that window, staring out, for a long time. It had been not long past midnight when they put me in there.

I heard the door open and looked behind me to see Charlie Silva come into the room, carrying a cardboard tray of takeout food and coffee.

"Early Christmas present," he said, setting it on the table. When I didn't move or say anything he said, "Come on, sit down and eat. Starving yourself won't help anything."

I went and sat across from him. He passed over a

container of coffee and some wrapped sandwiches. Scrambled eggs, bacon or sausage on a biscuit. He did unload several little cups of green chile to add some flavor, though. I took an egg and sausage sandwich and ate it with green chile, then one of the bacon ones. And, since Charlie wasn't eating them I had another after that.

"Well. That's better," Charlie said. I felt my face getting hot, and he smiled. "I used to run the YCFA campouts for the church—I know how much kids eat. That's why I brought so much. Have you been out of here since I left?"

He meant had I been out of the room. He knew I hadn't left the building.

"No. Have you seen Dad?"

"Yes. I saw him."

"Yeah, but, I mean, did they let you talk to him?"

"Sure."

"Is he okay?"

"Yes."

"Charlie, what's going on here? What are they planning to do with us?"

"They decided last night to hold all the juveniles till their parents or legal guardians picked them up."

"My dad came."

"Sí, pero, he's not your legal guardian, heh? You stay here till David E. Campbell picks you up."

"Hell could freeze over first. What about Dad?"

"They will hold him till after this Campbell arrives, too."

"Then what?"

Charlie shrugged and sipped at his coffee. I went back to the window and stared out some more. I had been hungry, but now that I had eaten something it was all just sitting like lead in the bottom of my stomach.

"Why don't you tell me about it?" Charlie said.

"There's nothing to tell."

"You think you're fooling anyone, refusing to talk? They faxed the whole police report down here from Iowa; we already know the story. One side of it, anyway. Why don't you tell me the other side?"

When I didn't say anything, he said, "Your daddy told everyone the law located him to raise you after your mama died. I take it that's not the case."

I turned away from the window again, leaning up against the sill. "No. I never lived with my mother. The way I hear it, she was in college when she had me. She didn't want a kid, so she gave me away to her sister to raise. Her sister didn't much want me either. Dad did. So, I'm living with him now."

"According to the police report, you didn't come home from Little League practice one day about five years ago. When your parents — excuse me — the Campbells, called your coach, he said you'd been knocked cold when some kid hit the ball clear up over the backstop. He said you seemed to be all right after, but he was worried about you, so he sent you home with the assistant coach."

"The assistant coach wasn't there," I said.

The assistant coach never showed up, but there was this guy called Jim who hung out watching practice all the time and helped the coach sometimes.

Damn. I hadn't thought about that in years.

"The description in the report is a man, probably Italian, about forty-five to fifty years old. Five feet seven inches tall, one hundred and seventy pounds, gray beard, gray hair, dark glasses."

"He wore colored glasses and padding and put some gray stuff on his hair when he was hanging out there."

"Your dad?"

"Yeah."

"What happened, Coyote?"

"Coach put me in that guy's car, and we drove off. Only we didn't go home."

When we left the parking lot of the school where practice was held, "Jim" went up the block and around the corner, then pulled in at the Dairy Queen and turned to look back at me.

"Head hurt?" he asked.

"Yeah."

"I got some Tylenol. You want some of that?"

"Yeah," I said. Never take medicine from a stranger, right? Coach trusted him though, and Mom gave me Tylenol all the time. He opened the glove compartment and pulled out a Tylenol bottle that had a few pills left in it. He shook one out, passed it back and handed me a paper cup of warm Gatorade to wash it down. Then, at his suggestion, I lay down on the seat as he drove off.

It didn't occur to me for some time, but it was taking us an awful long time to get home.

"Are you lost?" I asked him.

"No, not now. I took a wrong turn at the Dairy Queen. We'll be there in a minute."

I had the impression of driving forever, but that was because I was lying back there with my eyes shut, I figured. My head stopped hurting and I felt drowsy and next thing I knew, I was dead asleep.

Never take medicine from strangers.

Old rodeo man like Dad, he had some prescription painkillers left over from his last bad fall. Codeine tablets, which he kept for convenience in an old Tylenol bottle. By the time I woke up again, we were in another state.

"Coyote?"

"No," I said.

"No, what?"

"You can't lock him up for taking me away from there, Charlie. That was five years ago."

"It was still illegal."

"He's my father."

"Legally, no. Legally David Campbell is, and when your dad took you away from him, that was kidnapping."

"Campbell's not my dad!" I shouted at Charlie. "He was never my dad! Sure, when I was a little kid, I thought of him as my dad, but he's just the guy who happened to be married to my mother's sister. My own father found me and took me away to live with him. That's not kidnapping!"

"You know it is, Coyote," Charlie said softly. His hands were shaking, I noticed. Too many cups of coffee since last night. Charlie hadn't gone home yet, either.

"Don't you understand?" I said. "Maybe by law it wasn't right. Maybe he should be arrested for what he did. If you break a law, you have to be willing to suffer the consequences. How many times have I heard that line myself, huh? But he shouldn't have to suffer for something I did!"

"You didn't do anything."

"*I* got arrested, didn't I? *I* started the fight at the

bar. Dad was just telling me to stay out of trouble, and I went and punched out Joe Gallegos."

He just sat there, looking at me. Calm, quiet. I couldn't even tell if he understood what I meant or not; he didn't give any indication at all. I turned my back on him and stared out the window again.

"If the cops picked Dad up on their own, if you suspected something and checked the files—if anything like that happened and Dad ended up in jail, well, we'd both be sorry, sure. But he shouldn't have to pay for *my* mistake. If *I* put him in jail, it's different. Don't you see? That's just not something I want to have on my conscience for the rest of my life."

"Yo entiendo, sí," Charlie murmured softly. I understand, yes. "No wonder you stayed up all night pacing. *Pero,* you shouldn't worry about it. They probably won't press charges, if it's a custody thing. They don't, always."

"They do sometimes."

"Maybe we can talk to this Campbell when he shows up."

"Not when. If. I could die of old age waiting here for Dave Campbell."

"He's on his way," Charlie said.

"Wishful thinking."

"I talked to the man myself, Coyote. Last night. He seemed very worried about you."

"You found him?" I asked. "How?"

Charlie gave me a long, slow, thoughtful look, brushing his mustache with a knuckle. "Police records," he said finally.

"Our old address would have been on those reports. He doesn't live in Davenport anymore. He doesn't live anywhere in the whole Quad Cities area; he hasn't for at least four years."

"How do you know?"

"Come on, Charlie! What did you think? Some guy I don't know scoops me out of a ball field and says, 'Listen, kid, we never met, but I'm your real dad and you're coming to live with me now,' and I'd just say, 'Sure, fine, Buddy. Whatever'?"

I tried running away a couple times, but when we were traveling with the rodeo it was impossible. There were too many people helping him watch me. After his accident it was different, though. The rodeo people moved on, and we stayed. We were in Arizona when Dad got hurt. He was going to die, I thought then. I was certain of it. He was going to die, and I was going to be left all alone. There was no one else, no relatives on Dad's side of the family. Just the mother who had given me away. And the Campbells.

How long had it been since I had pushed them all to the back of my mind? Months at least. My family.

"If they wanted you back, they'd have found you by now," Dad had said, lots of times. "They're probably breathing a sigh of relief right now that you're gone. What did you think? That they really wanted you? If they did, they'd have adopted you a long time ago. Even if I let you take off now, you probably don't have anywhere to go. I bet as soon as they realized you were gone, they moved to another state so you wouldn't be able to find them."

I'd missed them before. There were times when it almost made me sick how much I missed them. Dave and Becky Campbell. Mom and Dad for the first ten years of my life. Mom and Dad. And Cecilia. Dave and Becky's daughter, five months my senior, but she was my sister. We were a family. They wouldn't go off and desert me like he said. They loved me. Suddenly, I wanted more than anything to go home again. Just go home.

I went to a change machine that was standing next to a bank of vending machines, got five dollars' worth of quarters and took them to a pay phone. Only, I didn't remember the number. I called information and discovered there were five David and two D. Campbells listed for Davenport, Iowa. I wrote them all down and, pumping quarters into the phone, I started calling.

I had to get more quarters. I had to call information

again. They weren't in the Davenport directory, but maybe they'd moved. Maybe they were in Rock Island now, across the river. Or Bettendorf, or Moline. Eleven assorted D. Campbells for the other three of the Quad Cities, but none of them were looking for a boy named Will.

I didn't cry. I hadn't cried since... well, over a year by then, anyway. But I remember feeling very small and alone. And scared. I wasn't ready to give up, though. I figured maybe the phone was unlisted for some reason. The fact is, they could still be living there, in the same house, on the same street, in the same town, but with a new, unlisted phone number. By morning, I knew Dad was going to live. He'd never ride rodeo again, but he was going to live. He planned to retire to his cabin in Monte Verde, and while he was in the hospital, I was going to stay across the road at the Delgados'. At least that was his plan. I had spent the night remembering my other family, though, and I had another plan. I wanted to go home.

Before I got on the plane to fly back to New Mexico, I wrote a letter and mailed it:

> *Dear Mom and Dad (and Cecilia),*
> *I am fine, but I miss you all very much and I want to come home...*

I gave them Sal Delgado's name, address, and phone number. I used Sal's address for a return address. Lucky thing, or I might never have known what happened to that letter. I got it back two weeks later, marked: "Return to sender. No such person at this address."

"I forget the name of the town," Charlie said. I had forgotten he was still in the room. "It was in the same state though. Iowa. The capital city."

"Des Moines?"

"I think so. That sounds right."

So. They didn't move out of the state. Just halfway across it. Something like a hundred and fifty miles.

"I bet as soon as they realized you were gone, they moved... so you wouldn't be able to find them..."

"Things aren't like they used to be," Charlie said to the ceiling. "People don't stay in the same house forever anymore. Gilly Ramon's people were neighbors to my family for six generations, but he's selling out and moving to Albuquerque now that his kids are grown and gone. City people, they move all the time. Bigger house, better neighborhood, new job in a new town. They all look the same, cities. People move here and there, it's all the same to them."

Was that supposed to be comforting? I didn't know.

But I did remember what it was like to be twelve years old, scared, alone, and living with strangers, and to realize the home I had always dreamed of getting back to wasn't there for me anymore. Maybe never had been.

FOUR

"Coyote. Wake up. He's here."

I sat up, blinking in the sudden light. It was dark outside. I looked up at the clock, wondering if it was Sunday yet, but it was still Saturday. I'd spent the whole day just waiting in that same room. It must have been about eight-thirty at night when I finally stretched out on the couch to take a nap, and by the clock, I'd been asleep less than twenty minutes. I think I'd have felt better if I hadn't slept at all.

"Who's here, Charlie? What are you talking about?"

"Tu daddy," he said. Your dad, in his typical English-Spanish mix. I stood up at once.

"Where?"

"At the front desk, signing you out. You can go home now."

Home. I sighed, relieved. It was over. Probably Dave

Campbell had told them just to leave me where I was. I didn't have to worry about Dad anymore because we were both going home now. I thought, *Man, Rex will be starving.* If I don't go feed him soon, he's going to eat somebody. I picked up my jacket and my hat and followed Charlie downstairs to the same area we'd all been held in last night after the fight. I looked around, but I didn't see Dad anywhere. There was a guy standing in front of the desk signing something, but he was a *gringo,* nobody I knew.

"Where?" I asked Charlie again.

Charlie answered by jerking his head, pointing his chin toward the desk. I looked again. Dad still wasn't there. Then the *gringo* guy turned around. He looked at me. He looked at Charlie. Charlie nodded. He came across the floor toward us, all the time staring at me. He was a tall man, over six feet, long-legged and lean, with fair hair that was beginning to thin on top and a long, sad face, despite the silly grin that was plastered over it just then. His eyes—light blue behind tinted flyer's style glasses—were wet with tears.

"Will!" he said. He came up to me with his arms out. "Will, thank God!" His arms went around me, grabbing me in a sudden, almost violent hug, and as he hugged me, he started to sob.

It was David Campbell.

"You said my dad was here," I told Charlie. Dave had gone to the rest room, either because he was so overcome with emotion or because he needed a pit stop after more than eighteen hours on the road.

"He's your dad," Charlie said, nodding toward the rest room.

"You know he's not."

"One of the girls I raised was my granddaughter, not my daughter. She had a different daddy somewhere else, but that didn't matter to me. She was one of my daughters, still is."

"Charlie . . ."

"Legally, you belong to him. He came a long way to find you, now he will take you home."

"Home, where?"

"Where he lives. Iowa."

"I'm not going," I said.

"You will get in the car with Mr. Campbell and drive back, or I will have a pair of deputies handcuff you and escort you back."

"Yeah? What about Dad? If you all got together and decided that legally I belong to Dave Campbell, then you have to believe my own dad kidnapped me. That's an automatic twenty-five years federal time. He can't go to prison, Charlie. Not for this. I thought you understood that!"

"There will be no charges."

"None?" I thought, *please let that be true,* but I was suspicious. It sounded too easy.

"None. Provided you go back with Mr. Campbell."

"Oh."

"Your face is too easy to read, Coyote. So, you go home, then you run away, come back here, heh? Don't even think about it. You going back is only one of the provisions. The other is that your father has no more contact with you. He cannot write to you, call you, nothing. Any contact or any attempt to get you back and the charges will be brought up. Like you said, twenty-five years."

I just stared at him. I felt my mouth hanging open and closed it again.

"Oh, man," I said softly. "You sewed us up good, didn't you? Was that your idea?"

Charlie sighed. For the first time since I had known him, he looked all of his seventy years.

"I helped negotiate it, yes. Mr. Campbell was pretty mad when he came in here—he wanted to see your daddy strung up by the thumbs at least. I talked him out of it. I knew how you felt about that. I arranged a deal. So, you tell me I'm wrong, Coyote. You have to go back, you have no choice. You want to go back knowing your daddy is okay, or knowing he is in jail because of your fight?"

I didn't answer that. I stood up and walked away, stood staring at a bulletin board full of wanted posters and community notices till Dave came back. He talked for a few minutes with Charlie Silva, then came and clapped me on the back.

"Let's go, Son," he said, smiling at me. "Let's go home."

Charlie stood next to me, waiting for me to do something. I put my hat on my head and turned toward the door. There was nothing else I could do. Nothing. Charlie had seen to that. But, walking out that door was a lot harder than walking in had been last night. Walking out meant walking away from my entire life. Walking away from my dad, from Dana, the cabin and Rex and San Pablo, Cipi, Bobby, Cody. Jesus, just from everything! *Fixed it, did you, Charlie? Damn you,* I thought. *God damn you.*

Dave Campbell's car was a sports car. I had to practically crawl into it, it was so low to the ground. When we both got in and got settled, he turned and smiled at me.

"It's so hard to believe..." He stopped, sighed, smiled again. "Well! Shall we go?"

"Whatever," I said.

"Let's see. Marshal Silva suggested the easiest way out of town would be down Rodeo Road. Is that this one in front here?"

"That one." I pointed across Cerrillos to the road that ran east past the mall, straight toward the mountains.

"Rodeo Road, then. Let's go."

"Yeah. Right."

I felt trapped. Helpless. But I was tired, too. It was late Saturday night, almost nine o'clock. I hadn't had more than that twenty-minute nap since I woke up Friday morning. The hum of the engine, the flash of passing streetlights, and the glare of oncoming headlights were hypnotic. I was asleep before we reached the Interstate on the far end of Rodeo Road.

It was dark. There was a scent of automobile upholstery in my nose, a flare of neon and fluorescent somewhere behind me. Someone's hand was on my shoulder, shaking me.

"Will! Will, wake up!"

A stranger was leaning over me, smiling. Fear flooded over me. I thrashed out to knock the hand away and toppled over off the car seat, onto the pavement below. Fortunately it wasn't a long fall. I blinked and looked up to see Dave Campbell leaning over me, worried now, no longer smiling.

"Will? Are you all right?"

"Yeah. Fine," I said, and went about getting myself up off the ground. Waking up like that had shaken me more than I was going to let him know. Exactly like that other time! I hadn't thought about that in a long time; now the memory was almost more real than what was happening now.

I had felt groggy and nauseated, waking up from a heavy, drugged sleep. The codeine was wearing off and my head was pounding, making it hard to think straight. Someone was leaning over me, shaking me as I came awake slowly in the back seat of a strange car.

"Billy! Billy, wake up!"

It was dark, the nighttime punctuated with bright spots of fluorescent lighting. I had no idea where I was or how I got there.

"Come inside," the stranger said.

"Come on in," Dave Campbell said.

I slammed the car door and started to follow him, up the step from the parking lot to the concrete walkway in front of the motel doors. One door was standing open, the light on inside, waiting for me. Halfway through the door, I stopped, turned and looked around. But the car at the curb was still a red Karmann Ghia. It hadn't changed into a battered old white Chevy, any more than I had suddenly become ten years old again.

I looked inside and thought it could be the same motel.

Sleepy, uncertain, I had followed a familiar voice. I could remember having been hit on the head with a baseball. "Jim" had driven me home. I was inside before it soaked in that this wasn't home, nothing like it. I looked up then, to see a standard two-bed motel room and by the time I realized that, the door behind me was shut and bolted.

"No," I said out loud. Not again. Not twice, for God's sake!

"Will? What's the matter?"

"Where are we?" I said.

"A motel," Dave said with an apologetic-looking smile. "I meant to head straight for home, but I was more tired than I thought. I didn't get too far. Let's go in and get some sleep."

"Let's not," I said. I had a feeling that if I stepped through that door I would be stuck in something I couldn't get out of. Again.

But, I was already stuck. Charlie had seen to that.

"I can't drive any farther, Will. I've been on the road since just after midnight and I'm exhausted. We'll leave early tomorrow, I promise."

I was in the room before he said anything, though. Dave followed me in and stood in the middle of the floor, yawning and stretching.

"Well," he said. "Here we are."

"Yeah."

"Will, I..."

"I'm tired," I said.

He frowned. Then he nodded. "Okay. We can talk later. I have to go make sure the car's locked up. I'll be right back."

"Yeah."

When he went outside, I undressed and climbed into bed right away. I had barely gotten under the covers by the time he got back, but I didn't want to have to make conversation, so I pretended to be asleep.

I was so tired, I felt dizzy, but sleep just wouldn't happen. I couldn't stop thinking. Dana and the dance and Joe Gallegos were swirling around in my head. Cipi and Sal Delgado, Bobby and Cody. Mom and Cecilia. Dad. Dave Campbell.

I remembered again how badly I had wanted to see him once. But Dad was right. When I needed him, he hadn't been there. He had no right, I thought, showing up *now,* arranging *my* life to his satisfaction, taking me away from my home, my friends, my family. No right.

But, the shock I had, waking up in the car like that right in front of a motel room, forced another memory on me. One I had put out of my mind a long time ago. Lying in bed in the dark, I recalled the slowly dawning fear I had felt on that other night, over five years ago, as I stood blinking in the light of the motel room, wondering what was going on as a strange man set a cowboy hat down on the bedside table and turned to face me.

He was small and lean with a thin black mustache and wide black eyes set deep in an angular face. I couldn't remember ever seeing him before in my life.

"Who are you?" I said. "Where am I? How come you brought me here . . . ?"

"One at a time, okay?" he said.

"Okay. Who are you?"

"You've been calling me Jim for two weeks. Don't you remember?"

Jim? Jim was a lot older than this guy and fifty pounds heavier. Then I noticed there was a bit of gray still streaking his hair and mustache and it looked like he just shaved a short while ago.

"How come you were wearing a disguise?" I asked. I was trying to pretend I wasn't scared, like maybe things like this happened to me all the time. But I was scared. I was terrified. I'd been warned often enough about kids getting kidnapped to know they almost never got back home afterwards.

"Billy, I want you to calm down. Don't be scared, Son. I'm not going to hurt you. I want to ask you something, okay? I'm just going to ask you a question."

"Then can I go home?"

I would not cry in front of him. I held my lip still from trembling, but the tears leaked out of my eyes anyway.

"I'm sorry," he said, and he reached out to wipe a tear off my face with his thumb. He had rough thumbs, the skin callused hard as wood. Jim's thumbs all right.

"I know it's scary, but I had to grab the chance when I got it. That ball hitting you was a stroke of luck for me. Anyway, what I want to ask you, did anyone ever tell you the Campbells are not your natural parents?"

"I knew that."

He looked relieved. "Do you know who your natural mother is?"

"Margaret Trevor."

"That's right. Margaret Trevor. Did anyone ever tell you who your real father is?"

"Uh. No." I didn't care. I had never cared. Dave and Becky Campbell were my parents, and that's all that mattered to me then. He reached into his jacket pocket and pulled out a folded piece of paper. He unfolded it and showed it to me.

"I want you to take a look at this," he said. "I don't intend for you to take anything on my say-so. Not yet. You know what this is?"

"No."

"It's a copy of your birth certificate. See the birth date here? That's your birthday, right?"

"Right."

"And see 'Mother's Maiden Name,' that's Margaret Jane Trevor. I guess they decided to let you know that much anyway."

"She's Mom's younger sister."

"Yeah? That's good. So, you've been living with family all this time. Now, look here. See where it has the space for 'Father's Name'? It says 'Guillermo S. Melendez.' That's me. Bill Melendez."

"Not Jim?"

"No. Now. Let me show you something else. Hang on."

He reached into a hip pocket this time and pulled out his wallet. He opened it, pulled out his driver's license and handed it to me. I took it and studied it, mainly because doing what he wanted meant I didn't have to think about anything else, like how badly I wanted to go home.

It had his photograph, and next to the picture was all the other information. Address, date of birth. Name. The name was Guillermo Santiago Melendez; hometown, Monte Verde, New Mexico, just like on the birth certificate. Nothing else matched, though. The spaces for 'Father's Street Address,' 'Date of Birth,' and 'Social Security Number' were blank on the birth certificate.

"Do you understand, Billy? Do you see what I'm saying to you here? I know you're a little confused right now, and I bet your head hurts a lot, but look at it. I'm your father, Billy. Your real father. You understand? I've been sitting around that ballpark for weeks trying to figure out a way to..."

"Kidnap me," I said.

"No, Billy, no... Well, yes. Kidnap you. How else was I ever going to get to know you? I never even knew I had a kid till I uncovered this by accident. Maggie never said anything, never wrote..." He sighed and ran a hand back through his hair, then looked at me again and smiled. "So, here we are."

"Can I go home now?" I said.

"You don't understand, Billy. We're in Kansas. I can't take you home now. I'd spend twenty-five years in jail on a kidnapping charge if I took you home now. I don't intend to do that. I know this is hard for you and scary. But, Billy... I'm sorry... that's just the way things are going to be from now on."

"I want to go home," I said. He wasn't going to take me home, though. I had known that from the time I realized where I was, though I tried to pretend otherwise. The tears started flowing again, and my breath caught in my throat. Jim... Bill... whoever he was... put his arm around me and held me while I sobbed on his shoulder.

FIVE

When I woke up the next morning, I saw Dave standing at the foot of the bed holding my jeans.

"What are you doing?" I said.

"Nothing." He put the jeans down and picked up his car keys. "Get some more rest. You need it."

"Where are you going?"

"I have an errand to run. I'll be back pretty quick. Just rest."

I tried to go back to sleep after he left. I hadn't slept at all Friday night, and last night I'd lain in bed for hours just remembering things, so I was tired, but I couldn't sleep anymore either. What was he up to anyway?

I gave it up after a while and went to take a shower. The hot water felt good after a day and two nights in the same clothes and I spent a long time in there. When I came out, I decided to shave, too. It's not something I had to do often yet, but it had been a couple days, so I did it that morning. I was still standing in front of the sink, wrapped in a towel, when the door opened and Dave walked back in.

"Oh. You're up," he said. "Ready for breakfast?"

"Sure," I said. "Just let me get dressed."

"Well, here. I got you a few clean things."

He was carrying a Wal-Mart bag, and he tipped it up and dumped it out on the bed. Undershorts, socks, another pair of jeans, and a shirt all tumbled out. That's why he was looking at my clothes when I woke up: he was getting the sizes off the labels.

"I know you've been in the same clothes for some time now," he said. "I thought you could use something clean to wear."

The morning after I got hit with the baseball, Dad took me to the store right after breakfast.

"What are we doing here?" I asked him.

"Picking up a few extra things for you to wear. You left home in kind of a hurry, huh?"

"I have plenty of clothes at the cabin," I told Dave.

"We're not there though, are we?" Dave said.

I walked to the window and pulled back a corner of the curtain. Last night I had just assumed we never left Santa Fe. I didn't remember driving out of town, and Dave had apologized about stopping so soon. Last night I had too many other things on my mind to think much about it. But the street I saw outside was Grand, a main drag in Las Vegas, New Mexico, a town about an hour north of Santa Fe.

"I know it's not far," Dave said. "But, like I said last night, I was tired. Anyway, this will hold you for the time being. It's all the right sizes."

I picked up all the clothes, opened the door, and tossed everything out into the parking lot. Dave stopped smiling.

"Will..."

"I have clothes," I said. "I have everything I need. I don't want these things."

"I thought you understood last night that we were going straight home. You even helped me find my way out of Santa Fe..."

"I thought we were going to *my* home first. You drove right straight toward Monte Verde, then overshot by about forty miles! I don't want a bunch of gifts, I want my own stuff!"

Dave sat down on the corner of one of the beds.

"I'm sorry, Will," he said finally. "I didn't think of it like that."

"Yeah? Well, what did you think of it like?"

"Oh. A miracle," he said. "I don't know what happened to you when you were taken away from us. I don't know how you felt or what you thought. But I know how I felt." He looked away from me, his eyes fixed on the closed curtains at the window, but he seemed to be seeing something else, something a whole lot farther away.

"I don't know if you can imagine what it's like to have a son, a boy you raised with love and pride. Try imagining it. Then imagine having that boy just disappear one day, vanish without a trace. Nothing. No clues... Well, no good clues anyway. We did piece together enough of the story to know there was some old man hanging out at the Little League field, and that for some odd reason, your coach not only trusted him, but sent you home in his car. I could have killed him when I heard that. I pressed charges against him."

"It wasn't his fault," I said. "Dad would have found some other way if that hadn't happened."

"Maybe. But, maybe not. It was a stupid thing for the coach to do. Utterly inexcusable. Come on, Will, you read the newspapers. You know what kind of old men hang around ballparks trying to pick up little boys. You know—I hate to say this but—sometimes I felt it would have been a lot easier for us if you had died. It may sound awful to you, but if it had been disease or an accident, we would have known where you were, what happened to you. But when you just vanished there was all the uncertainty along with the loss. We tried to start a new life, but in the back of everyone's mind, every day, the questions were always there: Is he all right? Is he hurt? Is he scared? Is he alive? Five and a half years, Will. And we never knew. Till the night before last, when the phone rang in the middle of the night. The state police called from New Mexico to tell us they'd found you, that you were all right, that you were safe."

He pulled off his glasses, and wiped at his eyes, brushing away tears he couldn't stop.

"People whose kids disappear dream of getting a phone call like that. It's the hope that they cling to every day that they live. I got that call, Will. I got the miracle." He put his glasses back on and looked at me. "That's where I'm at right now," he said.

"Okay, fine," I said. "But I haven't been living in a vacuum the past five years. I have a life, you know? To just get in a car and drive off and leave it all behind — it hurts!"

He sat silent for a long time, thinking that over. "Oh," he said finally, nodding. "I see."

"Can we go back?" I said. "I know I have to go to Iowa with you, I understand the conditions. But couldn't we wait a couple hours? Maybe a day or two? Give me a chance to pack, get my life together..."

"No. I'm sorry. It's just too far to go back now."

"Forty miles? It wouldn't take an hour to get back there. We wouldn't lose that much time. We could make it up driving straight through tonight if you're in such a hurry, I could..."

He shook his head, interrupting me. "No. Okay,

maybe 'too far' was just an excuse. The fact is I don't want you to go back there. Not at all."

"Why?"

"It's hard to explain. It's just this feeling I have that I have to get you as far from there as I can, as fast as I can. I tried to take off right away last night, but I was too exhausted to get very far. I don't think I'll be able to really believe you're coming home to us until I actually get you there. What we can do, though, is contact Marshal Silva. He gave me his home phone number and told me to get in touch with him about getting some of your things like school records settled. Maybe he can help us get your personal things too."

"What about my personal *life?*"

"Look, I'm sorry it has to be sudden like this, but the fact is, you're leaving town. Today, tomorrow, or next week, it doesn't really matter, does it? You'll still be gone. We're not going back."

It was like hearing echoes: *"You don't understand, Billy. We're in Kansas. I can't take you home now..."*

I shivered, but I wasn't sure if it was because of the present, the past, or standing around wearing only a towel in a drafty room. I stepped outside. The heap of new clothes was still sitting on the sidewalk in front of the door. I gathered it all up again and walked into the bathroom to change.

The car hummed loudly on the Interstate. Every minute was another mile farther from home. I wondered if Dad was back at the cabin, if they had let him go right away. I kept remembering we were supposed to go get wood. How was Dad supposed to go get wood alone? Sure, you could hardly notice the limp when he was just walking, but a day of hard labor always left him aching and sore. He couldn't do it alone. He needed me.

"You're quiet," Dave said, breaking into my thoughts.

"Mmm."

"I know how you feel, actually. It's hard sometimes to talk to strangers, and after all these years, we are strangers."

"It's okay to be shy at first," Dad had said that first day on the road. "But don't worry. We'll get used to each other."

"Are you cold?" Dave said. "Want me to turn on the heater?"

"No. I'm fine."

"Tell me about yourself

"What do you want to know?"

"Oh, whatever. How are you doing in school? What other interests do you have?"

"I'm doing fine in school," I said.

"A's? B's?" Dave asked.

"Mostly A's. Got one B though, so I blew a four point 0 already."

"Whew! You'll be a good influence on Cecilia. She's always been lazy about studying, but it's been worse since she started high school. All those activities, you know. Band, cheerleading, clubs. I think she could find time to study if she wanted to, but it might cut into her social life. Are you involved in any school activities?"

"No."

"What sort of things do you enjoy doing?"

"I don't know. Lots of things. I wrangle horses, and work with John Henry Gonzales. He's a local contractor, builds just about anything."

"Do you like that sort of thing?"

"Yeah. You can learn a lot working with a guy like John Henry. It's interesting."

"But you don't like sports?"

"Not, you know, basketball and stuff."

"What kind of sports do you like, then?"

"Rodeo."

"Melendez was in the rodeo once, wasn't he?" Dave said. He said the name like it tasted bad, like he had to spit it out quick because he couldn't stand to have it in his mouth. Dad had always managed to say Dave's name without sounding like that.

"How'd you know that? Did you know him?"

"I knew of him. I knew where Margaret met him. She told us that when she asked us to take care of you. I didn't actually know him though. I just mentioned it since you said you liked rodeo."

"Yeah, well. We traveled with the rodeo at first."

"Really? All over the country?"

"Dad mostly worked what they call the Turquoise Trail rodeos: Arizona, New Mexico, the Southwest. We didn't go east much."

"But, that must have been an interesting life."

"It was okay."

"Why did you stop and settle down?"

"Dad had a bad accident. He had to quit."

"What happened?"

"It's a long story," I said.

"That's all right. It's a long road too."

I don't want to be here, I thought. *I don't want to talk about Dad, I want to see him. I want to go home, talk to Dana, shoot some pool with Cip, take Rex and San Pablo up into the mountains where the aspen trees are gold and the deer are fading from summer brown to winter gray. Easier not to think too much about it, though. Easier just to talk instead.*

I said, "Do you know how a rodeo chute is built?"

"No. I've never seen one."

"Well, the gate isn't across the horse's nose, it's across one whole side. To get them saddled, you work from rails along the back and the front—the gate—then stand on those rails and lower yourself down into the saddle. Dad was just getting settled on this one horse, and it started bucking in the chute. Which happens. But when he started to jump back up and stand on the rails till the horse was ready, some idiot who was real green panicked and opened the gate. Dad's foot was on the gate and when it jerked open, he fell sideways. The sudden shift in weight threw the horse off balance, and they both rolled out of the chute sideways, Dad first and the horse on top of him."

"And he lived?"

"Sure. But he broke his pelvic bone, and apparently, that's not one you want to go around breaking. Right after the surgery they weren't sure if he'd ever walk again, but he does all right now. Mostly."

"Then you two settled down in Monte Verde? Why there?"

"That's Dad's hometown. He's got family there that goes back something like two hundred and fifty years."

"Did you meet a lot of relatives you never knew you had?"

"A few distant cousins. Dad didn't have any close relatives. He was sort of the last of his line."

"Is that why he wanted a son bad enough to kidnap one?"

"I don't think that had anything to do with it."

We had left past noon and were still south of Denver when we stopped for the night at another motel. We carried what little we had up to a second floor room that looked out over the parking lot, and Dave yawned and stretched and turned on the TV.

"What kind of shows do you like?" he asked, flipping through the channels.

"I don't know," I said. Dad and I didn't own a TV. You couldn't get good reception up the canyon anyway.

Dave shrugged and turned it off. "Nothing good on Sunday anyway."

Sunday?

I had been thinking earlier that Dad would be out trying to get wood today, and maybe he was, but now that I thought about it I realized it had been *yesterday* that we were planning to go get wood together. Saturday. I had spent all of Saturday waiting around the police station. It was such a totally wasted day, I had more or less stopped counting it somewhere along the line, like it never happened. It felt like today should be Saturday, but it wasn't. Today was *Sunday.* I had promised Dana I would call her on Sunday.

"I have to call someone," I said. "Right now. It's very important."

"Who?"

"You don't have to look suspicious like that. It's not my dad. It's a girl, okay? I promised her I'd call her Sunday." I pulled back the curtain and looked out. There was still light left, but the sun was long gone. "It's probably too late now anyway. She won't talk to me. She'll kill me."

"I'm sure she'd understand, if you explain why you didn't call earlier."

"You don't know her," I said.

"Well, if she doesn't understand, considering these are rather special circumstances, then chances are she never really cared for you all that much to begin with, wouldn't you think?"

"I just said you don't know her! You never met her so how can you stand there and tell me what she thinks or what she should think! If she is mad at me, it's all your fault anyway!"

"I'm sorry," Dave said. "You're right, I don't know her. Go ahead and call. I'll . . . uh . . . go wash up for dinner."

He disappeared into the bathroom, and I called Dana's house, but it didn't matter anyway. Dana wasn't there. Or if she was, she'd told her little brother to tell me she wasn't, which meant she was mad at me, and I couldn't even talk to her to explain why I hadn't called earlier. Just thinking of it made my stomach hurt.

Dave came out of the bathroom and asked if I was ready to go out to eat.

"I'm not hungry," I said.

"Is anything wrong?" he asked.

He was joking, right? My whole life was back down the road somewhere because of him and he wanted to know if anything was wrong. I looked at him and wondered if I should explain how bad it hurt to know I'd probably never see Dana again, but I kept thinking, why doesn't he already know that?

"How about if I go pick up something and we just eat here," he said, before I decided whether to tell him or not.

I couldn't think of anything I cared less about than dinner, but when I shrugged, he smiled like everything was fine, picked up the car keys, and left.

After he was gone, I walked to the window and looked down at the parking lot, thinking of Dana. It wouldn't do any good to call back. If she had decided not to talk to me, she wouldn't change her mind that fast.

A pickup with a big horse trailer pulled in, catching my attention. The driver got out and checked the horses before going to check into the motel. Rodeo man, looked like. A roper or a bulldogger, if he was hauling around his own horses. I suddenly wished I'd gone out to eat with Dave instead of waiting here. With that stock trailer out there, right under the window, I couldn't help but think back.

In the rodeo, a man gets to the championships by earning the most prize money throughout the season. He does this by getting to as many rodeos as possible. That meant a lot of time on the road, jumping from place to place, sometimes even leaving in the middle of a long rodeo, like the one in Albuquerque, to ride somewhere else and hurry back for the next round. There were other guys we traveled with a lot, meeting them over and over. The Harpers in particular. Dad and Jack Harper were good friends, and Dad often left his gear with Jack's sister Rachel while he and Jack flew somewhere and back together. Rachel traveled with Jack to take care of his kids, Sue and Jody, and to home-school them so they could stay on the road with him all season. Made sense for Dad to make arrangements for Rachel to teach me, too.

I told her about Dad kidnapping me, first chance I got. But she just smiled and said, "That's all right, honey, it's all over now." I told Jack Harper and he stood and listened impatiently then said, "Yeah, sure kid. Now, go on. I'm busy."

I didn't understand it. When you're in trouble, you're supposed to tell an adult, right? Someone you can trust, like a teacher. I told just about everyone I met, but they all brushed it off; they even helped Dad keep an eye on me so I couldn't take off on him. I found out why, though, when I went shopping with the Harpers. There was a stamp machine outside the store, and it gave me an idea. I was looking through my pockets for change when Rachel came out to see where I had gone.

"What are you doing?" she asked.

"Buying a stamp. I'm going to mail a letter." I looked up at her. "I'm going to write to my mom and dad and tell them to come and get me."

She knelt down in front of me and took my hands in hers. "Come on, honey. You know they aren't your mom and dad. They were just an aunt and uncle you lived with for a while when your mom was sick. I know you love them and miss them and you miss your mother, too. But you can't keep going around making up these stories about your dad. It hurts him, and it doesn't help you at all."

"Stories?" I asked, but I was afraid I could guess what she meant.

"You know he already told us about it. I know it must have been hard when your mother died, and when something like that happens, you want to be around people you know, like the Campbells. But, they were just helping out. They couldn't keep you forever.

You belong with your father. I know you never knew him before, and this is kind of a strange life, but you'll get used to it. You'll see, we'll have lots of fun."

Which explained why no one seemed to believe anything I ever told them. Apparently Dad had warned them in advance I was a liar and not to listen to any of my wild stories. And why shouldn't they believe him instead of me? They'd all known him a lot longer than they had known me. No one was going to help me get home, then. In fact, they were all going to help him make sure I didn't.

I closed the curtain and turned around, but the motel room was as bad as anything outside. Last time I slept in motels was when we were with the rodeo. I tried to remember how much I liked the rodeo: the sounds, the smells, the excitement. But the memory of people I didn't even know watching me out of the corner of their eye to make sure I didn't run off kept coming back, too. That, and Dad's voice: *"If they had wanted you back, they'd have found you by now..."*

I thought of Dave and his "miracle." How hard could it have been to get a name off a birth certificate and track it down? Guillermo S. Melendez, Monte Verde, New Mexico, printed right there in black and white. Tracking down Dave to find me had to have been harder, but Dad had managed that in only a month or so after he got hold of the birth certificate. Dave hadn't managed it in five and a half years.

"If they had wanted you back..."

Why did he have to show up now?

"For a guy who's in such a hurry to get home, you sure are taking your time," I said.

It was after ten in the morning and we were just swinging on to the Interstate again.

"I wanted to get out of New Mexico," Dave said. "But I don't feel quite so rushed now. Anyway, this is nice, don't you think? We get to do a little sightseeing, relax, spend some time together."

"It's kind of nice, isn't it, that we get to spend this time together, getting to know each other," Dad had said our second day on the road. It took us five days to get from the ballpark in Davenport to New Mexico.

"I could help drive, you know," I said. "About the only thing I managed to bring with me was my driver's license."

"That's right," Dave said, and he looked over at me like he was surprised or something. "You're sixteen, aren't you? Even though you're sitting right here next to me, I have the image in my mind of a ten-year-old boy. You're not ten though, are you?"

"No."

He smiled. "You look like your Grandpa Trevor."

People used to tell me that all the time when I was a kid, because, even though I was short for my age then, I was already kind of solid-built. Grandpa Trevor was a huge, heavyset man. I had his stockiness, but not his height. I inherited my eyes from him too: dark blue. "Trevor eyes," everyone used to call them. The rest of me looked a lot like Dad, though. I had his height (we were both under five feet eight) and his straight, almost-black hair and sharp-angled cheekbones. My nose was long and straight, like his, and just happened (thanks to San Pablo) to have a bump in the middle of it, like his.

"Maybe in a while you can drive. After you rest a little," Dave added, as I yawned again. "You didn't get much sleep last night, did you?"

"No."

As if memories weren't bad enough, the sound of traffic had kept me awake too. Even the room made noises that bothered me, like this heater that would switch itself on every now and then. Dave didn't even seem to notice it, but I hadn't slept in a room with a heater in it since . . . well, since the motels we stayed at on the rodeo circuit. The sounds I was used to falling asleep to were the crackle of burning piñon and the howl of coyotes in the canyon.

"How long ago did you guys move?" I asked. If I didn't talk, I was going to fall asleep. I was tired enough to sleep in the car, but vague memories of nightmares made me want to stay awake.

"It was in June, right after school let out, uh... Let me think. Four years ago."

"So, it was a year after... after I left."

"Was it only a year? I guess so. Actually, part of the reason I decided to make the move was because of that. It was hard for all of us, being reminded continually of the little boy we didn't have anymore. Your mother never quite got over it, though. If we went to the Dairy Queen for an ice cream cone, she'd cry, because we used to take Will to get ice cream there. If we went to a movie or a restaurant, she'd cry because once she took Will there. It was way out of hand."

"Huh."

"And, I thought the change of scenery would be good in other ways, too. Your mother clung to Cecilia so tight after you disappeared that it scared Cecilia. It wasn't healthy. She never got to walk to school again. Your mother drove her every day. She hardly let Cecilia out of her sight. I'm not saying Des Moines is safer. It's probably worse. But it's different. New schools, new neighborhood, not a constant reminder. I think she'd have broken down completely if we hadn't moved."

That was a startling thought. Although Dad had insisted I refer to Margaret Trevor as my real mother, and Becky Campbell as just an aunt, the fact is, the only mother I had ever known was Becky Campbell. I could say "my mother" and mean Margaret Trevor, but in my heart "Mom" was always Becky Campbell. And Mom couldn't "break down." Mom had to be there, waiting with hugs and comfort, no matter what happened. It was a law or something, wasn't it?

"By the way," Dave said. "I've been meaning to ask you something."

"What?"

"Whenever he talked about you, Marshal Silva kept calling you something else. Something strange sounding..."

"Coyote," I said.

"Right. Coh-yoh-tay. What exactly does that mean?"

"It's the Spanish pronunciation of what most people call a kī-ōt. Coyote is a slang term for someone who's half Spanish and half Anglo. It's also my nickname."

"That doesn't seem like a nice thing to call somebody."

"Oh, I don't know. A coyote is a pretty tough animal. He's a survivor. Wolves got wiped out in New Mexico, but the coyote's still around. Even with no laws protecting them, they're spreading out into totally new ranges. Besides, I *am* half Spanish and half Anglo, so calling me that is hardly an insult."

"It still seems rude."

"The guy who started calling me that meant it to be rude. It backfired on him."

We stopped in Denver, where Dave wanted to buy some souvenirs and stuff, and then we wasted more time stopping for a late lunch.

While we were waiting for the pizza to arrive, Dave said, "There's something else that's been bothering me."

"What?"

"You were at a police station when I came for you. You were there because you'd been arrested in a bar fight."

"Yeah."

"Is that normal behavior for you?"

"I admit it looks that way right now, but it's not really. There's just this one guy at school that I've been having a feud with since the first day I moved in. I knocked him around a little about a week ago and Friday night, he was looking for revenge. It goes that way sometimes."

Dave was quiet for a minute while the waitress brought our pizza, and I poured more Coke out of the pitcher into my glass. I was thinking, too bad we couldn't have a pitcher of beer instead of Coke. Cokes (sodas I mean, any kind: Dad got me into the habit of calling all soft drinks "Cokes") are too sweet. It's kind of like drinking melted cotton candy sometimes. That's why I'll get a beer if I'm somewhere I know I can buy one despite the laws. They just taste better. I figured Dave would probably faint if I asked for a beer though. Anyway, he said I could drive after lunch. Cruising through an unfamiliar city in a strange car, buzzed out on beer, didn't sound like a real good idea.

"I don't agree with fighting," Dave said when the waitress left.

"I know. But Joe won't be at the new school, will he?"

"No. But you weren't at school when you got arrested. You were at a bar. I think that bothers me more than the fighting."

It took me a minute to figure out why it would. "I was at a dance."

"But why were you at a *bar?*"

"That's where they hold dances. At bars. Oh. I see what you mean. No, I don't go around hanging out in bars a lot. Well, Sal's Bar, but you can't count that because that's like Cipi's living room, and anyway, it's not a regular bar. They sell groceries there, and run the outfitting business from there. I mean, yeah, they sell drinks, but they sell tortillas too, things like that."

"They don't hold dances at the school?"

"Sometimes. But not too many. And I like to dance. Dancing is fun and bars just happen to be the only places around with dance floors."

He didn't get it though. He still sat there looking thoughtful. I had a feeling he was thinking I was a lot wilder than I really was. Seemed to me that Charlie Silva once said I gave that impression anyway, and I'd better watch it if I didn't want to get a reputation as a troublemaker. I'm not a troublemaker. I just can't stand Joe Gallegos.

"How late was this fight that interrupted the dance?" he asked after a while.

"I don't know. Ten, eleven, maybe. I wasn't paying much attention at the time."

"What was your curfew for the dance that night?"

"What do you mean? What time the bars have to close? I think it's two, but I don't know. I've never been out that late."

"That's something. But what I meant was what time were you supposed to be home that night? What did Melendez set for your time limit?"

"Dad never told me what time to come home," I said.

"He let you stay out as late as you wanted, whenever you wanted?"

"He had to know where I was when it got dark. But he didn't set many other specific time limits."

"After the rodeo accident, did he work at all?"

"Yeah. Almost all the time."

"I imagine that he normally got home much later than you got out of school?"

"Couple hours, anyway." It took the bus till after four to get all the way up the canyon where we lived, even though school let out at three. Most of Dad's jobs let out at five, and he was home between five-thirty and six. Construction jobs sometimes let out earlier and the lumberyard didn't let him off till seven, but on the average, I was alone an hour and a half every afternoon after school.

"What sort of arrangements did he make, particularly when you were younger, when you were going to be home before he was?"

"Arrangements? Well, the rule was whoever got home first lit the fires, took dry wood inside, maybe started dinner..."

"I meant who checked up on you? Who kept an eye on you?"

"You mean like who babysat me? Nobody. I don't need a babysitter."

"But you were miles away from town, without even a telephone. What if something happened?"

"Sal's Bar was right across the road. It was a very narrow road, too."

"That's not the same as having someone responsible for you," Dave said.

"I was responsible for me," I said.

Dave didn't look convinced. His attitude made me mad. He seemed to think I was a little kid who needed to have his hand held all the time. Or that I was running wild in the streets without his influence to keep me in line. Dave was the first one that taught me about responsibility. What did he think? I just forgot all that?

"Will . . ." Dave said.

"Look," I said. "Just how much longer is this trip going to take?"

"What do you mean?"

"I mean it's . . . what now? Monday afternoon? We left Santa Fe Saturday night. We could easily have been back by now and we're not even halfway. You said something about spending time together. I'm just wondering how much time. A week? Two? At the rate we're traveling, we could get there faster in a covered wagon."

"We are taking this trip pretty easy, I admit. But, I thought it would be a good idea for you to get used to things a little at a time. Get used to being around me again first, take things step by step and not just have to plunge into a new home, a new life, and everything all at once. It seems to me that we're doing all right. I can understand your hostility, but little by little you're starting to talk to me about things, how you feel and all. We had some good talks these past two days. That's progress, don't you think?"

"That's not progress, man. That's breaking me down by making me relive the worst five days of my life."

He looked shocked, then thoughtful. "Of course," he said finally. "I hadn't thought of that."

"You didn't ask, either."

"No. I didn't. It's not that I don't care; I'm dying to know every detail of what happened to you when you vanished and in the years since, but I don't want to pry. You'll tell me, I figure, when you're ready."

"Maybe."

He smiled. "All right. Good enough. You want to push this trip harder then?"

"Yeah," I said. "I do."

Just get it over with, I was thinking. *Just get there and get it over with.*

"Okay. Fine," Dave agreed. "We'll stop again tonight. We've taken too long already today not to. But tomorrow we can finish the trip in one long, steady drive. I'll call your mother tonight and tell her to expect us tomorrow evening."

SIX

"Home, sweet home," Dave said as we pulled into the driveway of a two-story house. It was about twice as big as the house I'd grown up in. I had a sudden stab of nostalgia, remembering the little story-and-a-half red-brick house with its deep yard, its border of lilac bushes, and the huge spreading apple tree in the back yard. This neighborhood was obviously a couple steps up, but it lacked the character that the old one had. And it lacked a feeling of home. I'd hoped we would at least be in a familiar type of territory. This was as alien as the log cabin had been the first time I laid eyes on it. Besides which, it looked deserted. Dave had called last night to tell them to expect us, and he spent half the drive today catching me up on family gossip: what all the cousins and aunts and uncles had been doing lately. I had kind of expected a bunch of them to be at the house, like a big welcome-home or something. If everyone was as thrilled as he said to find out I was back, why weren't they here to say hello?

"Uh, there's not anything big planned is there?" I asked, just to be sure. "I mean, like, people popping out from under couches screaming 'surprise' or anything?"

"No," Dave said. "There's just family tonight."

"Yeah, but... you have kind of a big family, don't you?"

He clapped me on the shoulder and said, "Time enough to catch up on uncles and cousins after you've seen your mother and sister."

"Get used to things a little at a time?"

"Some things," he agreed. "Come on in. They've probably been waiting all day."

I thought, *man, some homecoming.* He was probably embarrassed to have me back. I didn't say anything though, just followed him up the walk that led from the driveway to the front door.

As soon as he pushed open the door, I heard someone shouting, "It's them, Mom! They're here!" and the clatter of running feet on the stairs.

"Dad!"

Dave was caught up in a hug by a female person. It took me a minute to get a look at her. First she'd been moving fast, then she was half-swallowed by Dave's trench coat. Finally she stepped back and looked at me. She looked past me, like she thought there might be someone else back there, then she looked at me again.

"Cecil?" I said.

"Will? Is that you?"

"It's me."

"I hardly recognized you!"

"Yeah. Me, too."

I remembered her as a child with crooked teeth and spiky red hair that Mom always cut off short because she wouldn't comb it. I remembered a ten-year-old with legs like a stork, coming into her growth years before any boy would and lording those extra inches over me, making me wish I wasn't male, wasn't short for my age, wasn't five months younger—all the time tripping over her own feet because she wasn't used herself to their sudden size.

What I saw was a young woman, about my age, still a bit taller than me, but now with all of her in proportion to those legs. Long, smooth, round legs now, not sticklike ones. There must have been braces while I was gone: her teeth were perfect. And her hair was not red and spiky, but waves of loose strawberry-blonde curls. Her eyes were intensely blue. She had inherited the "Trevor eyes," too. I decided not to send any pictures of her back home for a while. Sister or no, Dana would freak if she saw who I was going to be living with from now on.

Shaking hands felt awkward. Being near her felt awkward. I should hug her, I thought, but I hardly knew her. Ah, what the hell. I hugged her. She looked surprised, then happy. She hugged me tightly back. And Mom walked into the room.

Five years had altered Dave only slightly, and had made Cecilia grow up. The same five years had been hard on Mom. She seemed tiny to me, probably because I was a lot bigger than when I last saw her. She was shorter than me now, and she'd put on weight. Her eyes were also Trevor blue, but they were lined with tiny, fine wrinkles. Her hair was cut short and plain, and was streaked heavily with gray. There was a set to her mouth that made her look unhappy. She stepped up to me as I moved away from Cecilia, and for a long moment she just stared. She reached up one hand and touched my cheek. She traced the line of my cheek and jaw, like she was looking for something. Then I noticed the tears in her eyes, welling up, finally spilling over. She started sobbing suddenly and fell into my arms. Nothing could have prepared me for the awful feeling of guilt that sliced through my heart at that moment.

Cecilia walked into the room without knocking and announced, "Dinner's ready." Then she stopped and stared at me. "What are you doing?" she asked.

I was sitting on the bed.

"Please tell me this room has not been like this since you moved," I said.

It was my room. Anyway, it was all the stuff I remembered from my room when I was a kid transported to a new, bigger room, in a new house, halfway across the state. All the old furniture, even the curtains and bedspread. I could still remember picking them out when I was about six years old. Blue, with spaceships all over them.

"No. This was Mom's sewing room. When Dad went to pick you up, Mom and I lugged all her stuff downstairs and brought this up out of storage for you. I told her you wouldn't like it. I told her we should go out and get new stuff. Everyone else got new stuff when we moved. But she wanted you to pick your own new stuff, so you're stuck with this till we go shopping."

"Oh, man," I said.

"I know, it's ugly, but..."

"I don't care what it looks like. It just feels weird, that's all." *I used to keep my baseball in the glove on the corner of that same dresser. A picture of all the team, with Coach standing behind us had hung over it. Coach had sent me home one night with a stranger...*

"Uh. You said dinner's ready?"

"Yeah. Mom fixed your favorite."

My favorite? Navajo tacos? *Chiles rellenos?*

Cecilia laughed. "Meatloaf and macaroni! Pretend like you're thrilled. She spent three days planning this meal. Come on. Let's go down."

I'd had the full tour as soon as I arrived. The house

seemed huge to me. Big rooms all over the place with broad windows, fancy carpeting and furniture. Nothing in the whole place was familiar — except the spaceships and some stuff thrown into the rec room in the basement that I realized used to be in our living room. Home, sweet home? Dave's maybe. Not mine.

Dinner was in the dining room. I never lived in a house with a dining room before. It was in the back of the house and from there a huge sliding glass door opened onto a concrete patio at the top of a back yard that was surrounded by an eight-foot high redwood fence. Step one, Cecilia explained to me. They had been saving up for a pool since they moved here. The law was that any pool bigger than a kiddie wading pool had to have an eight-foot fence around it. Last year they had built the fence. This spring they'd put in the pool. Next year they could put in a cabaña at the back corner of the yard. Whatever a "cabaña" was.

Mom apparently agreed with Charlie on how much to feed a teenager. We had baked potatoes with butter, green beans, corn, and biscuits besides the macaroni and cheese and Mom's homemade meatloaf.

Mom. I looked up as the name came to mind again and saw her across the table. Her eyes met mine and she smiled, and the years seemed to lift off like magic. God, I had missed Mom. I looked at Dave, but no magic happened with him. He had been my dad. Once. Dad was my dad now. I had two dads, but I only had one mom, one sister.

"Anything wrong, Will?" Dave said.

"No, I'm . . . uh . . . tired," I said.

"You're going to hate this school," Cecilia said, handing me the beans.

"Cecil!" Dave said.

"Well, he is. It's so disgusting. It's supposed to be like one of the newest schools in the city, but the roof leaks all the time."

"Once," Dave said with a sigh.

"It's a pretty big school," Mom said, partly I think to distract them both. Mom. I liked the sound of that. "There are several little suburbs on this side of the city and they all use the same high school. Some of the buses travel miles to bring kids in."

"The bus I used to take to school went twenty-two miles, and didn't go all the way to the end of the road," I said.

"Twenty-two miles? Is that how far you were from town?" Dave asked.

"No. We weren't the last stop on the line. Some of the buses went farther though. Santa Fe and Las Vegas are sixty miles apart, and there's only two schools in between. One of them only goes up to the eighth grade. Monte Verde is the other one."

"Then you must have gone to a pretty big school," Mom said.

"Yeah. Pretty big. There were eight hundred and twenty kids, if you include the Head Start."

"Head Start was at the high school?" Cecilia asked.

"No. I meant from Head Start through high school."

"You've got to be kidding," she said, rolling her eyes. "There's almost that many kids in the graduating class at this school."

"Yeah?"

"Almost four thousand kids total, and that doesn't include the Head Start, or any of the grade schools or junior highs."

Four thousand? The Monte Verde phone book, which included the village itself and all the surrounding communities, had less than a thousand names in it.

"The building is enormous," Cecilia went on. "They built it all on one level, so no one would have to run up and down stairs all the time. Brilliant, right? The main hallway, from the front of the school to the swimming pool, is a quarter of a mile long."

"Swimming pool?"

"Oh, yeah. We got everything. Pool. Two gyms, tennis courts, a huge auditorium. What else? Lousy football team. School band has won about every award available, though. You're a sophomore this year, right?"

"Junior," I said.

"Sophomore," Dave said.

"Junior," I repeated.

"Junior means eleventh grade," Dave informed me.

"I know."

"I haven't flunked anything," Cecilia said. *"I'm* in the eleventh grade this year. You've always been one grade behind me."

"I skipped one," I said.

Everyone at the table stopped eating to stare at me.

"You did what?" Dave asked.

"I skipped," I repeated.

Rachel Harper had been giving Jody simple work, catch-up stuff, because he was a bad student. When she finally noticed how bored I was with it, she gave me some tests and I ended up testing out of the fifth grade entirely.

"When was this?" Dave demanded.

"Right after I...uh...went with Dad. I've always been able to keep up, it's no big deal."

"You skipped a grade right away?" Dave asked.

"Yeah." I'd just said that, hadn't I?

Mom looked ready to cry. Dave reached out and patted her hand and said, "Done is done, honey."

Their attitude made me mad. "Dad was proud of me," I said.

"We are, too," Dave said. "It's just hard to track down a kid when he's been registered in the wrong grade."

"There's other ways," I said.

Dave opened his mouth again, but Cecilia interrupted.

"Anyway, I guess that means you'll be in my homeroom. They're assigned alphabetically and by grade. I doubt we'll have classes together, though. Ugh! What a thought! I *hope* we don't have any of the same teachers! If you're going to be one of those goody-goody types, getting good grades and all, the last thing I need is having some teacher tell me how I ought to take example from my baby brother...Hey, when are you starting, anyway? Tomorrow?"

"He just got here!" Mom said. "Give him a chance to get used to things before you rush him off again."

"Sometimes it is better to dive in head first than to take all day getting used to the water." Dave grinned at me. "What do you think, Will?"

"I might as well start tomorrow. I missed over a week of school already—I should get back into things."

"We've only been on the road for two school days," Dave said. "How does that figure to a week?"

"I was out Wednesday, Thursday, and Friday last week, too."

"Why? Were you sick?" Mom asked, looking worried.

Great, I thought. I'd just spoken up without thinking. Now I recalled why it was I'd been out of school. Yesterday I'd been assuring Dave I wasn't the type to get into trouble all the time. If I hadn't mentioned it myself, he might never have known about the suspension.

"Will?" Dave said.

"I . . . uh . . . had a little argument with another kid, and I ended up with a three-day suspension. Nothing serious."

"You were suspended for an argument?" Dave asked. "Or a fight?" Weird, I thought. Dad used that exact same tone of voice sometimes.

"It was a fight."

Dave sighed and looked away.

"Look, I don't go around picking fights with strangers," I said. "It was Gallegos. That was the fight he was getting revenge for when he came after me at the dance."

"You didn't turn into one of those macho guys that's always out to prove something, did you?" Cecilia asked.

"No. I just don't like Joe Gallegos. And it's mutual. But he's not here. Okay?"

Dave didn't answer. He picked up a fork and stabbed something off his plate.

"Oh, yeah," I said. "I'm real sorry if I didn't reach up high enough to meet your expectations."

"You don't have to meet anything," Dave said. "But I thought I taught you when you were little that you don't have to hit people to make a point."

"Yeah. I know. But there were a lot of tough kids in that school. I liked having a reputation as someone who'll finish fights if other people start them, because that way fewer people started things with me. Besides, sometimes it just feels good to whack someone like Joe Gallegos!"

Cecilia's sudden shout of laughter seemed to drain off some of the tension. I thought, *man, she hasn't changed a bit.* It was a warm feeling, but a strange one too. I *had* changed. I wasn't sure how I felt about suddenly being part of a family I hadn't seen since I was a little kid. It was all alien to me in some ways, frighteningly familiar in others. The house was strange, the town was strange. Mom and Cecil were like... coming home. Good and bad, all rolled into one big lump, and Dave...

I looked across the table at Dave again and saw him watching me. I felt like he was just sitting there, waiting for me to do something wrong. Like he expected it.

"Uh," I said, trying to remember where the conversation had gone wrong. "If I can get started, I mean, my records probably aren't here or anything, but I would like to go to school as soon as I can. Tomorrow, if possible."

"You don't have to go yet if you don't want to," Mom said.

"He can make up his own mind, Becky. In fact, it sounds as though he already has. Tomorrow is fine, Will."

"Okay. Great."

I did want to go to school, if for no other reason than just to get out of this house for a while. There was too much going on here, too many things too fast; it was confusing. I needed some space.

It should have occurred to me that school is not exactly a relaxing environment.

SEVEN

I was assigned a counselor by the name of Mr. Lawson to help me arrange a class schedule. He was a lanky, sandy-haired guy with a habit of staring, unblinking, into your eyes all the time. It's supposed to show interest when you stare at someone's eyes. But his eyes were so dead that it was like trying to stare down a lizard. It made me nervous, so I kept looking away, which he probably took as a sign that I had a guilty conscience. He asked questions about what classes I had already taken, since there were certain ones required for graduation, and he wrote me out a schedule. They had seven class periods at this school. I had economics first period, math second, Spanish third. At least two semesters of foreign language were required, and I hadn't bothered to take anything like that before. Russian, German, French, and Latin didn't much interest me, so I opted for Spanish. I figured it would be an easy grade: I already knew Spanish. Fourth period I had study hall on Monday, Wednesday, and Friday and PE on Tuesday and Thursday.

"PE has first lunch," Lawson informed me. "That means you go to lunch right after third period, and you go to the gym after. For your study hall days, take first lunch if you go to the library. If you sign up for a learning lab with a teacher who has a free period, find out ahead of time what lunch to take."

Fifth period I had biology, sixth was another study hall, this one every day instead of part-time. Seventh period was an English class, composition or something. It was halfway through second period before he got all that figured out and, at his suggestion, I spent the rest of the period roaming the halls with the map he had given me, locating my locker and all my classes.

It wasn't bad, for a first day. But the first day at a new school, you spend most of your time getting lost, getting books, and a list of assignments from the teachers.

There isn't time for much on the first day. It passes in a haze of confusion. I knew this from experience. Same thing had happened when I started at Monte Verde. Dad's accident was late in September, so my first day was about a month into the new school year. Like now, I was the only one stumbling around wondering what was going on. In a way, I figured this was a little easier. This time at least I knew what to expect, what high school was all about. In Monte Verde, the kids were divided into three sections: Head Start, grade school, and high school. The first six grades were grade school, everyone else was high school. So I didn't have middle school in between, just grade school, a year of home study, and bam, high school. This school was enormous, like Cecilia had said. The masses of kids pouring into the hall every time the bell rang were a little scary. But I figured, I can do this. That was the first day, though.

The second day was less confusing, but that didn't make it any better. First off, I had to go introduce myself to the economics teacher, Mr. Yates. He took my admit slip, wrote my name down, handed me a book and a seat assignment, and then went right into the day's lesson. I tried to follow the lesson, and at the same time glance back through the book to see what I'd missed. I hadn't had an economics class before. I was curious as to what it was all about. But, trying to do two things at once was only part of the reason I almost blew it.

"So, who knows the answer to that? How about you, Mr. Campbell?"

We seemed to be on chapter two, which had to do with banks.

"Mr. Campbell? Earth to Campbell? Is anyone there?"

I realized that someone in the class was in trouble, and I looked around, only to find everyone else was looking at me.

"That is your name, isn't it? Campbell?"

I almost said "No," till I remembered that now it was. "Yes, sir!"

"So glad you could join us, Mr. Campbell. Next time I plan to call on you in class, where should I leave a wake-up call?"

He had to be a comedian, right? He couldn't just get mad or something simple. Campbell. At least last time I started a new school, I knew what my name was supposed to be by the time I went there.

Math was no problem. I was already farther along than the class I got transferred to. And Spanish. Then, according to Mr. Lawson, I was supposed to go to lunch and report after first lunch to the gym. I did that. No one else was walking toward the gym. Just me. When I got there, no one seemed to be around the two gyms or the boys' locker rooms. I found a wrestling class finally, upstairs in the mat room, taught by a fat, bald guy wearing a T-shirt that said "Coach."

"What are you doing here?" he demanded when I came in.

I gave him the admit slip.

"This is dated yesterday," he noticed.

"Yes, sir. I started yesterday."

"Then why are you late today?"

"This is what time I was told to come here."

"You got gym fourth period, you come here at the end of third period, don't you? Where were you when the bell rang?"

"I went to lunch."

"You went to lunch?"

"Yes, sir."

"Is that what they did at your old school? Just take off and go to lunch anytime they felt like it?"

"No, sir."

"Then why'd you do it here?"

I really wanted to tell him off, but I've dealt with guys like him before. You try to argue back and they just get worse.

"I was led to understand that PE took first lunch, and that I should eat, then report here," I said as politely as possible.

"Well, you were led wrong, Son. You should have come up here and asked. Get your facts, don't rely on rumors." He turned away from me for a moment and blew his whistle. "All of you hit the showers!" he hollered, and he turned back to me again as the other boys filed out. He didn't just turn back, he turned and studied me, from my boots to my hair. He didn't seem to like what he saw. I still had only the two changes of clothes, and they were pretty much the same: boot-top jeans and a western shirt, cowboy boots, and a belt with a buckle that had a picture of a cowboy throwing a rope at a running calf. Anywhere in New Mexico, no one would have given me a second look. More non-cowboys dress cowboy out there than the real ones. Here though, it wasn't exactly the height of fashion, and I'd noticed already a good number of odd looks from the other students. I didn't really care what people thought of my clothes, but I didn't like the way this "Coach" person was sizing me up either.

"Getting ready for the big costume dance at the end of the month, are you?"

"No, sir."

"People who try to be different are usually trying to make a statement, Campbell. What kind of statement are you trying to make with that outfit?"

"Only that my luggage didn't travel east as fast as I did. Sir."

He stood there, tapping his fingers on his clipboard, trying to figure if that was a smart-aleck remark he could get me into serious trouble for or not. Finally he decided it was too borderline to push. Yet.

"I never want to see you wear those boots on that cork floor downstairs," he said instead. The big gym, instead of hardwood, had some kind of soft surface on it. "You understand me? You got some reason to walk on my floor, you take those boots off."

"Yes, sir." As if I was the only kid in school who wore boots! I wondered if he said the same thing to pretty girls like Cecilia who wore spike-heeled shoes to school. Not too likely.

He looked through the papers on his clipboard. "We started the new six weeks over a week ago."

"I'm sorry. Six weeks of what?"

"Activity. This six weeks we have wrestling, archery, basketball, and football. Take your pick."

I had no idea what he was talking about, but I said "Basketball." At least I knew the rules to basketball.

He scribbled something unintelligible on my admit slip and said, "Take this down to Coach Kittering." Then he turned his back on me and left. I had an urge to wad up the slip and throw it at him. I wanted to smack him with it right between the fringe of gray hair on the back of his neck and the top of his T-shirt where a fat fold of flesh stuck out. Pointless though. And not worth the trouble it would get me. I left the mat room and went looking for Coach Kittering. I found out when I did that all the gym classes except wrestling *did* take first lunch. I came early is why I had trouble finding anyone at first.

"How was school?" Mom asked when I got home.

"How is school ever?" Cecilia answered for me, coming in the door behind me.

"I was talking to Will, dear."

"School sucks," Cecilia said. "Will told the homeroom teacher to call him Billy," she added. She really hadn't changed. She still answered my questions for me and tattled in the same breath.

"Why did you do that?" Mom wanted to know.

"Because people have been calling me Billy for five years or so, and I don't always remember to answer to anything else."

"Carol Markham told me you got into a lot of trouble in economics today," Cecilia added. "Said you smarted off to the teacher."

"I didn't smart off to the teacher," I said.

"Why would Carol Markham say that if you didn't?" Mom asked.

"I don't know Carol Markham, so I couldn't say, but I didn't smart off to anybody today. Not even to Coach Childress, and he damn well deserved it."

"Ooooh, Childress has a bad rep, man, watch out for him," Cecilia warned me, belatedly.

"Did you have some problem with Coach Childress?" Mom asked.

"No."

"Because I could speak to him . . ."

"No! It's fine. Everything is fine!"

"He's sure touchy," Cecilia said, as I went upstairs to get away from the conversation.

I didn't have much to do upstairs, though. I'd done all my homework in study hall. I sat by my bedroom window for a minute, looking out at other upstairs windows and across a sea of dropping rooftops to a view of the freeway. Sounds rose up to me, the sounds of the suburbs. It wasn't so different from the sounds I used to hear on a fall afternoon when we lived in the old house, in Davenport. I could hear the muted roar of traffic from the freeway below, the random shouting noise kids make when they're playing, the hum of a lawnmower, the slam of a basketball on a concrete driveway. Strange and unfamiliar to me now.

I thought of my bedroom in the cabin, of the windows that looked out at the river valley below. I recalled the sigh of the wind in the tops of the ponderosas, the scream of it howling up and down the canyons in the spring, the dead silence of snow falling on a still night. I remembered the sound of rain pounding on the tin roof, and the *thunk* and scamper of clawed feet as a squirrel dropped out of a tree onto the tin, the sound of Rex howling in answer to the coyotes in the canyon.

I was homesick. I'd spent the day trying to blank out my old life and work on getting used to the new one, but it wasn't all that easy. I couldn't help but wonder what Dad was doing, how he was. Did he think of me? Did he wonder what I was doing and how I felt, or did he think I wanted to be here? I didn't want to go back to school tomorrow. I wanted to go home.

No chance, though. I did the next best thing. I sat down at my desk and wrote another letter to Dana, my fourth one since I left home. I borrowed a stamp from Mom, refused her offer of a ride, and went for a hike to post it myself. I had to get out of the house, away from the easy familiarity of a girl I barely knew, away from a mother, lost and found and unknown, away from everything. Just for a while.

It was a long time since I had walked city streets. The houses parked on the green lawns were closer together than I remembered houses as being in this part of the country, but maybe I was looking back on things with a child's perspective. Maybe the huge lawn and acre of garden I remembered was just another little city lot like all of these. It didn't seem possible, but last night, a box of pictures had been hauled out and shown around, and there did seem to be a house right behind our back fence, where I remembered there being a forest or an orchard at least.

I found the mailbox, right where Mom said it would be, and paused to read the pickup hours before slipping my letter in the slot. It was Thursday afternoon. I had mailed my first letter to Dana on Monday. Surely she had that by now. Surely she understood by now what had happened and how I felt. When would I get a letter back? Not till next Monday, probably. Monday seemed a lifetime away.

Walking back, I passed a corner lot where a man was sitting in the middle of the back yard with a broad piece of white paper spread out in front of him and a heap of what looked like wood scraps all around.

"Hi," I said.

He glanced up, grunted a greeting, and went back to studying the paper.

"What is all that?" I asked, because it looked like it was supposed to be something, and I couldn't figure out what.

"Kit to make a doghouse," he said, and made a gesture with one arm toward the side. I looked and saw a little fat puppy tied with a rope to the clothesline post.

"I made a doghouse once," I commented. "Never heard of getting a kit for one though."

"Well, it looked like a good idea when I saw it in the lumberyard," he said, tossing the paper down in exasperation. Since he seemed friendly, I walked up onto the grass, and looked over his pile of wood and his white paper plans.

"Not much of a blueprint, is it?" I said.

"Not much of anything," he agreed. "This is probably one of those stupid things a five-year-old is supposed to be able to put together, and silly me, I forgot to pick up a five-year-old with the glue and nails."

"Well, it can't be that hard," I said. "I suppose you should start by separating all the wood. Then, even if you can't figure out the plan, you can slap it together with whatever you have."

We did that. He had some pieces of one-by-two for the bracing. On Rex's doghouse I'd used two-by-fours. Of course, Rex was a monster compared to this guy's pup. Rex was a big, ugly red mutt that looked to be part Airedale, part Irish setter, and part German shepherd, among other interesting things.

There were precut slabs of quarter-inch-thick paneling for the walls. I'd covered Rex's house with half-inch plywood. There were two sheets of quarter-inch particle board and some pieces of roofing to cover the top. Rex's doghouse had half-inch plywood for a roof, was shingled, and was insulated with broken pieces of

Styrofoam. John Henry Gonzales gave me the shingles and insulation since he had some left over from a job I had helped on.

Building was something I could do, and no one here was yelling at me about my choice of footwear, or asking me about wake-up calls, or making me do anything else I didn't want to do. So, I stayed and helped. The plans never did make much sense. I pretty much put the thing together the way I thought it should look, with the kit's owner helping mostly by holding things and passing nails over. In only a couple hours, we were admiring the finished product.

"Looks better than the display model they had in the store," the man said. "At least you nailed it together instead of just gluing it."

"They usually don't put a lot of effort into those displays."

"I guess. You're pretty handy to have around though. Live around here?"

"Up on Hawthorne, halfway up the block. I just moved in a couple days ago."

"Ever built anything besides a doghouse?"

"Oh, sure. Where I used to live there was this contractor who liked to hire kids in the summer. I worked with him a lot."

"I was thinking of buying a kit to build a redwood deck out here this summer," he said. "Maybe you could give me a hand with that, too, time comes."

"I'd be glad to." I gave him my name and Dave's phone number and said, "Anytime you need help, give me a call."

"I'll do that. What do I owe you for this afternoon?"

"Nothing."

"Now, you did a lot of work here today. There's no way I could have gotten all that done so fast alone."

"Maybe. Anyway, it's not like you hired me to help, I offered. I can't accept payment for that. Besides, I had fun. I like building things."

"Well, okay, then. If I get around to that deck though, I'll hire you for that. Seems to me you did a lot better on this doghouse than the carpenter I hired did on my back fence."

"Deal," I said, and shook his hand. I felt better, walking the last block and a half home in the dusk, kind of like I'd accomplished something. The way I came here, the things that had happened since, all made me feel sort of helpless, like I wasn't in control of myself anymore. A simple thing like meeting a new person and slapping together a doghouse made me feel more in control again, more like myself. Then I got home and Dave hit the roof.

"Where on earth have you been? How long can it take to mail a letter? It's not half a mile to the mailbox, and you've been gone for hours! Don't you realize how scared your mother has been, wondering where you were, what happened to you..."

"I didn't mean to scare anybody. I said I was going for a walk..."

"For three hours? Did you say anything about being gone for three hours? Will, we were worried sick."

"It's just now getting dark. I always come home before dark."

"You always *came* home before dark, maybe, but this is a different house, a different set of rules. You can't just take off and vanish without telling anyone where you are, then pop up again when you're ready. We have to know where you are all the time, how you plan to get there, what time you intend to come back. How can we tell if anything's wrong if we don't know what's happening?"

"I'm sorry. I was just up the street. I didn't think it was that big of a deal."

"It is that big of a deal. Will, please understand, we lost you once, remember...?"

"Yeah, but I'm sixteen years old now, for crying out loud. I can take care of myself."

"That one never works," Cecilia said. "I've been trying it for years."

"Cecilia, go to your room," Dave said.

She sighed theatrically, gathered up a stack of schoolbooks, and walked off. It always astounded me how much racket someone as graceful as Cecilia could make walking out of a room. Not that she was always noisy. Just when she wanted to be sure people noticed her.

"Will..."

"Look, I'm sorry, all right? I can't cancel out what already happened, all I can do is be sorry."

"And not let it happen again."

"Right. By the way, can I get a job?"

"A job? What kind of job?"

"I don't know. Whatever kind of job there is to get. I'm used to a little more labor after school. I'm kind of bored."

"I don't think that's really necessary, Will. There's plenty around here that needs doing, and I want you to get used to your new schedule before you try taking on more responsibilities. What you need to do is make some new friends, not to spend the rest of your life laboring for room and board."

"Is that what you think? That Dad made me work for my room and board?"

"I didn't say that."

"It sure sounded like it. Yeah, I had chores at home, but I do here, too. They're just different, that's all."

"Will, I know this is all new to you, and it's going to be hard to get used to. But this is home now, not 'here.' This is home and..." he hesitated, then said, "and I'm your father. I wish you could try to get back into the habit of calling me that. You still call... Melendez...'Dad,' and everytime you do that, you're shutting me out, cutting us off before we have a chance to get to be family again."

"I know you're used to calling your Uncle Dave 'Dad,' Billy," Dad had said the first day after I found out who he really was. "But I'm your father. I don't expect you to start calling me your dad right off the bat, but start getting used to the idea, Son. We're family now."

I felt like the walls were closing in on me. I needed to get out. "Can I go for another walk?"

"No. It's time for dinner now."

I wanted to hit something. I wanted to kick something. I wanted to yell at him to leave me alone. What I did was go upstairs and wash up for dinner.

EIGHT

"I'd rather just wait for my stuff to come from ho... from Charlie Silva," I said.

"You have two outfits, Will. You had to stretch them between three days of school already. That can't go on."

"You *did* write to Charlie, didn't you?"

"I did," Dave said. He climbed into the driver's side of the car, and leaned to unlock the other doors. The Ghia was Dave's car. Mom had a station wagon. We were taking the station wagon because everybody was going. It was Saturday and we were having a family day at the mall. Dana, I remembered, liked to hang out in the mall. I took her there a couple times after I got my truck, but I was reminded as we walked through the shops of a line in a Louis L'Amour novel: I never saw so much stuff that a man didn't need in all my life. The idea of a day in the mall didn't exactly thrill me.

"Why is it," Dave asked, "that you always refer to Marshal Silva as 'Charlie'? It seems to me a man of his years and station deserves a little more respect from you."

"Everybody calls him 'Charlie,'" I said. "He's been the law around there so long, half the town calls him 'Uncle Charlie.'"

Dave didn't answer that, but I could see he still didn't think it was right. I'd have to remember that too, I supposed. Start calling Charlie "Marshal Silva" as if he was a stranger instead of a man I had known for years. Like I had to remember not to refer to the place where I'd lived for the past four years as "home," and the man who raised me for over five years as "Dad," and to answer when people started hollering at "Will

Campbell" instead of answering to the name I'd used for the last third of my life.

Cecilia and Mom came out, finally, and climbed into the car.

"All set?" Dave asked.

"All set," Mom agreed.

"Doors locked?"

"Yes. We're ready. Let's go."

I'd been locked out of the house once already. They'd issued me a key, but I kept leaving it on my desk. I hadn't had to deal with locked doors since the motel rooms on the rodeo circuit. I don't even know for certain if the cabin door had a lock. If it did, we never used it.

"I'm glad you could join us today, Cecilia," Dave said, a little sarcastically.

"Wouldn't miss it," she grinned back.

"I thought you didn't like going to the store with your poor, antiquated parents."

"Actually, I don't," she said. "It can sort of cramp your style, right, Billy? In case I meet someone who's nice—and cute."

"Billy?" Dave asked.

"Sure. That's what they call him at school." Cecilia shrugged.

"If parents cramp your style, don't parents and a brother make it worse?" I asked.

"Maybe it could. But what I'm figuring is that I should be seen in public as often as possible with you *and* my parents so that people will realize we're family, see? Then, if I talk to you at school, the guys won't think you're, like, competition."

"Right," I said. "Thanks."

"Besides, this should be interesting. I mean, how many people are there in the world who have only two pairs of pants and two shirts? We're talking complete makeover here, total wardrobe replacement. I have to know how much all this costs in case I ever want to do it myself sometime."

"There was a time when you were growing so fast we had to start over from scratch every six months," Mom said. "Thank goodness those days are over."

"Where do you usually buy clothes and stuff?" Cecilia asked.

"K-Mart or Wal-Mart, or Franklin's Home and Ranch Store. For dressy shirts I usually go to Cooper's Western Wear in the mall."

"If that box of clothes ever shows up," Cecilia said, "let's hide it from him and burn it when he's not home. You know there's already kids at school who call you 'The Farmer.'"

"I'm not a farmer. I'm a cowboy."

"That's worse. Those rodeo guys are cruel to animals."

"I never did understand where people came up with that," I said.

"They torture them," Cecilia told me, "to make them mean so they'll buck."

"That's not true. Rodeo horses are some of the best-cared-for horses in the world. There was a grand-champion bronc just a year or so back that retired at the age of twenty. You won't find a racehorse that old. Even most saddle horses are in the glue factory before that."

"Yeah?" she said. "If they're so loved and everything, why are they so mean?"

"You got it backwards. Horses aren't mean because they're in the rodeo; they go to the rodeo because they're mean. Horses have dispositions, just like people. I know one very well, in fact, that's a top trail horse, but he's so ornery only a good rider can use him. He seems to think he's carnivorous, too. Give him a chance, and he'll take a chunk out of you."

"Well, they still shouldn't chase those little cows around and throw them down like they do. That seems awfully cruel."

"You think that's cruel," I said, "you should see what we do to the stock you eat before you get it."

"Like what?" Cecilia challenged.

"First you chase them into a narrow iron slot, so you can work with them without having to rope them and tie them down on the ground like in the Old West.

The slot has a gate in the end and you slam it and catch their neck in it so they can't get away."

"Well, I suppose they have to have some way to hold them still," Cecilia said.

"Yeah. Then you get red-hot iron and burn a mark into their skin."

"I've heard that doesn't really hurt," Dave said.

"Tell it to the cows. I've done it to them and believe me, it hurts. They wouldn't yell like that if it didn't. Lovely odor too."

"Don't you give them Novocain or something?" Cecilia asked.

"You're kidding, right? Anyway, the branding's the easy part. Then you take a sharp knife and cut notches in their ears. The brand's not legal without the proper ear notch. Then you get your knife again and go around to the back end and throw some Lysol on them for disinfectant..."

"Uh, Will," Dave said.

"Personally," I said, "I think a cow that grows up to go to the rodeo is better treated than one that grows up into a Big Mac."

"I think I'll become a vegetarian," Cecilia said.

"Well?" Dave asked.

"I don't know," I said. "Is this how they're supposed to fit?"

He straightened up from where he'd been leaning on the wall as I came out of the dressing room and studied the new jeans. "I think so. It looks like every other kid around here. I wish our womenfolk hadn't run out on us; Cecilia's a much better judge of current fashion than I am."

"It doesn't matter," I said, retreating again. "I can't wear these."

"Why not? They look fine to me."

"They don't feel right, though. Everybody's bugging me that my clothes look silly. But these *feel* silly to me. I'd rather dress different than the average kid and feel like myself than match everyone else and feel like a freak."

I came out in my own jeans and handed the ones I'd been trying on to the girl behind the security counter.

"In a few weeks, you might feel differently, and wish you did look a little more conformist."

"I don't know. Do you think I'm a conformist type?"

Dave studied me seriously for a long moment, then gave me a grin. "I think there is a western wear store in this place. Shall we go have a look?"

It had a different name, but it was a lot like Cooper's in Santa Fe: familiar. I picked out a couple of pairs of boot-cut jeans and a couple shirts.

"You need more than that," Dave said.

"My things'll be coming soon, won't they?"

"I hope so, but that's still not much."

"I only wear one outfit at a time and you...we... do have a washer."

"How about something more dressy, too? Do you have a suit?"

"No. I never needed a suit."

"Did you ever go to church out there?"

"I wore jeans to church, just like almost everyone else in town, male and female."

"You're being stubborn about this. Stubborn even for you, and you've always had a mulish streak. Are you afraid that if you get new things, you won't get your old things back, that I'm trying to trick you somehow?"

"No."

"What is it then?"

"It just doesn't feel right."

"What doesn't?"

"This. All of it. You're spending an awful lot of money, buying me things that I don't really need."

"It's not that much, and you do need it."

Talk about stubborn. Was he evading the point on purpose?

"Will?"

"One of the things you made me leave behind was my bank account, okay? I came out here with only the cash I had on me at a dance, just enough to buy a few glasses of Coke at mixed-drink prices. I have my own money for things like clothes and movies and all that. I don't like this feeling of . . . I don't know. I feel like a poor relation."

"Is that why you wanted your own job?"

"Partly."

"You told me you weren't in the habit of paying your own room and board, but that's what this sounds like to me. I don't know how you've been living, but I feel a family is responsible for the support of its children while they are still children. I buy all of Cecilia's clothes and necessities. She has an allowance, not a fortune, but an allowance, to buy things that she wants besides that. I don't see any reason to treat you any different. Are you telling me you're in the habit of supporting yourself?"

"No."

"Buying all your own clothes and personal items?"

"No. Not really."

"Then why does it bother you?"

Because I don't know you! I wanted to shout. Because it's not like family, it's like taking gifts from a stranger. Because I want my own things back, I don't want them all replaced. Again.

"I don't know," I said. "I guess it shouldn't."

"I want you to get a suit," Dave said. "Do you want to get one here, or at a more conventional store?"

"I'll get something here, if it's not too expensive."

I didn't pick a suit-suit, though. I picked out a western sport coat and a dress shirt that I could wear with jeans. Dave let it go at that.

"How big a bank account are we talking about?" he asked when we went to check out.

"I just bought all new tires for my truck, but I think I have about five hundred and fifty left, around there. The truck and the new engine I bought to put in it took a big chunk out, but I was planning to build it back up working next summer."

"Build it back up for what?"

"College," I said.

He looked surprised, and that made me mad. What did he think I was saving up for? Another truck? I guess he thought that since Dad didn't go to college, he would try to talk me out of going, too. Dad didn't go because he couldn't afford it. The only reason he let me buy that truck was he knew I would make it up again during school holidays.

"Monday, we'll open you an account at the local bank, and then you can send your account number to wherever your old account was and have them transfer the funds over to you," Dave said.

"Where my old account was, it takes twenty-five dollars to open an account."

"If it makes you feel better, whatever it costs to open one here, you can pay me back."

"All right. What about my truck?"

"That we'll discuss later."

"Yeah?"

"Yeah."

NINE

I had to be careful to keep up with the work in economics because Yates seemed to enjoy calling on me in class. My math teacher couldn't believe some kid from a little bitty country school could possibly know such advanced math as he was teaching, so he had me do the problems on the board more than any other kid in class. My Spanish teacher said I spoke Spanish with the strangest accent she'd ever heard, and I had better get over my habit of slurring words together, like for instance be careful to enunciate *"para qué..."* instead of saying *"pa' qué..."* though I never heard anyone speak Spanish that way in my life. In PE, Childress kept his eye on me, even though he was supposed to be teaching a different section than I was in. I decided, too, that I should have thought longer before choosing basketball. I was playing against kids who were six and a half feet tall. One kid was taking basketball in gym for an easy grade. He was on the school team, and he stood seven feet even. I am not kidding. I hadn't felt short for a long time, but he made me feel like a circus midget.

I wrote to Dana every day, checked the mail every day for answers from her, from the guys, from anybody. I was beginning to wonder if the mail was getting through. Maybe someone had made a deal with the post office not to deliver any letters from me. Could they do that? I was beginning to think they could.

Between school and dinner were all the empty hours I normally filled up with chopping wood, roping practice, helping Sal Delgado and anyone else who needed a hand, and hanging out with the other Canyon Cowboys. I had no friends here, refused several invitations to go to the mall or other such interesting places with Cecilia, hated TV. I cleaned out the garage one afternoon, did enough trim work in the flower beds to last it till spring. I raked up the puny pile of leaves in the yard every day, raked leaves for any of the neighbors who wanted it done, tuned up both Mom's and Dave's cars, washed all the windows on the house and garage. It wasn't enough, though. I was still homesick.

Mom made appointments for me with the dentist and the doctor. I guess when you get a new kid you have to check him out, like test driving a new car, maybe. The doctor thing was after school one afternoon, but the dental checkup was in the morning. I came in late and took my excuse note to the office to get a pass to go back to class.

There was someone else coming in late at almost the same time, a girl. I waited behind her at the office window, not paying much attention one way or another till the lady in the office said, "I can't find your name on my list. You're in the tenth grade, right?"

"Yeah." She stretched up on tiptoe to lean in the window and read the list herself upside down. "There it is," she said, and giggled. "Dana Rodriguez."

Dana Rodriguez?

She had her pass already, and as soon as her name was crossed off the list, she walked off down the hall. All I could see then was her back, a retreating figure in a loose shirt and jeans, with long dark hair. Dana Rodriguez. What a coincidence to have a girl going to this school with the same name as the girl I was in love with. My Dana was about the same height, darker, a lot rounder in build. Still, how many Dana Rodriguezes were there in this whole country in the tenth grade? Not that many, I was sure.

"I said, can I help you?"

I realized I'd been staring for a long time, and, flushing, I handed my note to the lady at the window.

I mentioned the incident in my letter to Dana that

night. It had been a week and a half since I wrote my first one to her, and I still had no answer. But, I wrote another one, and considered asking Dave about the possibility of another long-distance phone call. Mail in Monte Verde was not a real consistent thing. Dad joked that they still delivered it by burro. Some days it seemed to go all right, some days the burro was sick. Maybe I should try to call her again.

Thursday I saw the new Dana Rodriguez again, just after the last bell. I'd been cutting through the student center, on my way to the bus concourse at the other side of the school, and I saw her head out the front doors. The buses waited awhile for everyone to get their stuff together and get out there, so on impulse, I turned and went back the other way, out the broad glass doors to the parking area at the front of the school. She was standing near the curb, balancing her books on her head. Waiting for a ride, probably. Why else would she be out there, killing time like that?

I hadn't gotten a real clear look at her face before, but I was sure it was the same girl. She was kind of short, wearing loose men's overalls and a baggy flannel shirt that made it totally impossible to see what she looked like underneath. Her hair, I could see now, wasn't just brown like I'd thought, but a sort of red-brown, like an old penny, and it hung clear down to her waist. I thought of my Dana's jet black curls and round soft body. Then, following another impulse, I walked up to this one.

"Excuse me," I said.

She tilted her head forward just enough to make the books slide off and caught them perfectly in her hands, turning at the same time. "Why? Did you burp or something?"

"Uh. No. I meant, excuse me for interrupting you."

"Oh. Okay." She turned away again.

"Uh..."

"Did you want something?" she asked, turning back.

"I just uh...thought I'd...come over and meet you. I guess. I was behind you the other day in the office, when you were getting a late pass..."

"Yeah. I remember you."

"You do?" I was surprised. I didn't know she'd even looked at me.

She laughed. "Sure. There's not that many cowboys in our school, you know. Very boring place here, generally. So. You thought we should meet because we both have problems getting to school in the morning?"

"No. It was just that I noticed you had the same name as the girl I was dating before I moved here, and I thought it was an interesting coincidence."

"Yeah? You knew a Diana Rodriguez somewhere else?"

"Di . . . ? Your name is Diana?"

"Sure. What'd you think it was?"

"Dana."

"Dana is a guy's name. You know, like that old actor, Dana Andrews."

"The girl I knew was named Dana."

"In my case it was a typo on the absent list, that's why the lady couldn't find it. They dropped the 'i'. Maybe your girlfriend dropped her 'i' somewhere, too."

"Uh. I don't think so."

"Well. You know. There's an actress named Glenn Close, and one named Michael Learned. So, I guess you can have a girlfriend named Dana."

"Thank you. You're very generous. Well, I guess this makes the entire day a total waste of time. Not that it made much sense in the first place to come over here and introduce myself just because I know someone with the same name as yours, but since you don't even have the same name after all . . ."

"She must be kind of special."

"What?"

"This Dana. If you wanted to meet me just because you thought I had her name, she must have been something special to you."

"She still is."

"How long ago did you move away from wherever it was that you knew her?"

"A week ago Saturday."

"Oh! Pretty quick then. What's she think about letting a cute one like you get away?"

"She . . . what? I mean, I don't know. It was very sudden, this move. I didn't get a chance to tell her about it till after I was gone. She hasn't answered any of my letters yet."

"Mad at you, probably. I would be if my boyfriend moved away and didn't tell me till he was gone."

"I didn't have a lot of warning myself," I said.

She looked skeptical. But then, it sounded stupid, even to me.

"You realize, don't you," she said, "that you know my name, but I don't know yours?"

"It's Billy Melendez," I said. Damn! I was going to have to start thinking before I opened my mouth. "Will Campbell. Uh, Billy Campbell."

"Do you do that for everybody, or just me? Keep making up new names till you hit one you like the sound of?"

"It's not me," I said. "It's the people around me. My father has one name for me, the uncle I live with now another."

"Oh. Yeah, I see what you mean. It gets confusing. Like, my mother's name is Velarde now. It was Muñoz when I was born. My grandmother's name is Rodriguez, and I live with her, so I'm a Rodriguez. It's easier that way."

"Yeah," I said. Her eyes, I noticed, were the same shade of old copper as her hair.

"So. Are you out here waiting for someone, too?" she asked.

"No. I . . . I just stopped out here to say 'hi.' I have to go catch the bus."

"School bus?" she asked.

"Of course." What other kind of bus would I need to catch just then? "Why?"

"'Cause the buses just left," she said, pointing. The buses came out a side street on the north side of the school and turned onto the main road east of it. We were on the south side of the school, facing east, and there they went, a whole line of buses, some going east, some north, some south.

"Damn!" I said. I threw my books down on the ground, and considered sending my hat down after them.

"You live a long way off?"

"Ah, not that far. Probably just barely inside the bus limits. But my parents freaked the other day when I stopped to help some guy down the road. I miss the bus and they'll be having heart failure in seconds."

"Why? Kids miss buses sometimes."

"Yeah, well, they're always worried I'm going to get kidnapped or something."

"You real rich?"

"No. I guess they think about it a lot because it happened before," I said, gathering up my books. When I stood up, I saw her looking at me with interest.

"You've been kidnapped?" she asked.

I felt my face getting red. I realized I'd told her enough to make her curious, and I didn't feel like making long explanations to a total stranger, even if she was sort of fun to talk to. "It was one of those custody things."

"Oh! That's why you had to leave town so fast you never even got to explain to your girlfriend, right?"

"Right."

"Are you kidnapped now, or were you before?"

"Sometimes it's hard to tell the difference." I sighed. "Mom is gonna freak."

"Why don't you go back in and call her, and when my cousin shows up here, if he ever does, he can give you a ride home."

"That's real nice, but I'm sure if someone's coming to get you, you've got an appointment or something, and it's probably not even two miles. I can walk it."

"I don't have an appointment. My cousin comes to pick me up every day after school. He brings me, too."

"Sounds like my sister. Have you ever been kidnapped?"

"I don't think it's kidnapping my grandmother's worried about. I think it's rape or something. I had to argue with her for a year to let me go to public school instead of the Catholic high school. We finally had to compromise: I can go to public school, but I can't use public transportation. So, my cousin gets out of school—at the Catholic school—and comes to pick me up every day. Silly, huh? He wouldn't mind taking you home, though. Unless you live way out in the middle of nowhere, on one of those farms west of here."

"No, it's not far."

"He'll be here soon. Go on in and call and I'll have him wait if he gets here."

"Okay. I will. Thanks."

I called Mom and explained why I wouldn't be on the bus in case it got there before I did. When I went back outside, there was a car pulled up next to the curb where Diana was standing. It was a very old Chevy with leaky valves and the splotchy rust-orange and gray color of a car that's still waiting to be primed for a new paint job. When I walked over, Diana introduced me to the driver, her cousin Rodrigo Montaño. He was maybe eighteen, tall, and skinny with long, ratty black hair and a wisp of mustache on his upper lip and he looked half asleep.

When I leaned in to shake his hand and said, *"Como te 'ido?"* he seemed to perk a little.

"Bien. Vamos, hombre. Pa' donde vas?"

"Mi casa 'sta en un camino que se llama Hawthorne. Know where that is?"

"Nope. You can show me."

I crawled in the back, and Diana sat up front with her cousin. The car belched a big cloud of blue smoke, then eased out of the parking area.

"East, to Twenty-second," I said. "I can find it from there."

"Bueno," was all he said. Not a real talkative type, I could tell right off.

"Listen," I said. "Just out of curiosity. Are there a lot of Spanish people around here? I thought it was pretty much all . . . you know. White, upper middle-class. That sort of thing."

"Lot of that, yeah. Couple black kids in this school. Couple guys from our neighborhood, most of our girls go to the Catholic high school though. That's why I decided to go there."

"What neighborhood is your neighborhood?"

"Down by the railroad. Lot of *gringos* down there too, but there's a few like us. Spanish. We're Spanish. There's some Mexicans, too. You don't talk like someone who learned Spanish here," he added, flipping a finger at the school building we were leaving behind.

"I learned in New Mexico. Half of my family is from New Mexico."

"The Melendez half?" Diana asked, grinning at me.

"Yeah. The Melendez half."

"Right on. Our neighbors have relatives out that way. So, you're new to this part of the world?"

"I was born near here, but I haven't been here for years. I just moved back less than two weeks ago."

"Suddenly," Diana added. "Under the cover of darkness."

He must've been a real cousin. He seemed used to her, didn't even pay attention to her silliness.

"You like it out here?" he asked me.

"No," I said. "I don't even want to be here, but who asked, right? At first at least I was busy getting used to things, but now... *Yo no sé.*"

"You bored, man? If being busy's all it takes to make you happy, man, come out to my place this weekend. We're building a garage. My dad can cure boredom fast."

"You serious?" I asked. "I'd like that."

"You would?" He looked at me in the rearview mirror to see if I was crazy or something.

"I used to work construction jobs in the summer. When I wasn't wrangling horses or herding cattle. I kind of like building things. Beats cleaning the basement just for something to do."

"Hey, it's a date then, man, I'll pick you up. The more hands there are, the less work I have to do."

"Sounds good to me."

"Loco," he murmured, and we got to Twenty-second, so I gave him directions to get to the house. He said he'd come by around eight Saturday morning, and I shook hands on that, thanked him again, and went inside. It wasn't so stupid after all, introducing myself to that girl. Now I had a new friend. Two new friends, really. Diana was all right, too. Maybe it was possible to survive all this after all.

Saturday, I stood by the front door and waited till eight-fifteen, then out of boredom I started raking the leaves out of the front yard. Again. The Chevy drew up in front of the house around nine-thirty, and Rodrigo just sat there while I put the rake away, grabbed a jacket, and went out to meet him. I was kind of irritated he was so late, but I didn't want to say anything about it. I asked him though if they had started without me.

"No, man, we haven't started nothing yet," he said. It was easy to believe. Rodrigo leaned back, one arm in the window, one hand lying loose on the steering wheel as if he were too tired to drive. His eyes were half-shut and he moved like in slow motion. Driving home from school in the middle of the afternoon like that was one thing, but cutting in and out of Saturday morning shopping traffic, I wished he was a little livelier. Fortunately, he was headed mainly away from where most other cars were going.

His neighborhood had lots of big houses, old ones, though, with gardens in most of the back yards, not pools. Rodrigo parked on the street in front of a weathered-looking white house with a deep, covered porch that ran across the entire front. He turned off the car and, after resting a moment, shoved open his door and slouched out into the street. I got out on the curb side and waited for him to come around, which he did, eventually.

I followed him to the side of the house, where there was a driveway that led back to a newly poured slab the size of a single-car garage. It was back there where I met Rodrigo's father and two other men who'd come to help out. Nine-thirty in the morning, and they were all standing around drinking beer. Soon as we got there, Rodrigo helped himself to a cold one and offered one to me, but I shook my head. I liked the taste, sure, but John Henry had taught me that beer and construction work don't mix. He said beer on the job was a good way to end up slicing off a finger, or something more important.

I don't think I so much as broke into a sweat all day. There was a lot of talk, a lot of confusion, a lot of beer.

By the time Mrs. Montaño brought lunch out for us a little past twelve o'clock, we'd proceeded all the way up to having half the boards cut for the back wall of the garage. John Henry would have had a fit if his crew ever worked that slow. Of course, these were homeowners, not construction contractors, but I like to come away from a project with the good feeling of having accomplished something, not with a sense that I'd just wasted a whole day.

Everyone was real friendly, but after getting congratulated several times on my grasp of the English language, I came to understand that there were no neighbors from New Mexico, there were neighbors from Mexico. Rodrigo, among others, didn't understand the difference and I gave up trying to explain further than saying I was in fact American, and had spent most of my life right here. Don't they teach American geography in the public schools anymore?

We got one wall framed by sunset. One. John Henry would have had us working till midnight if we hadn't gotten all four framed, standing, and tied together. At this rate, no way the Montaños would have a garage by the first snowfall. I walked around in the fading light, picking up loose nails and rolling electrical cords while Rodrigo joined his father and uncles for another couple beers. They asked if I was coming to help tomorrow, and I told them it was hard for me to get away on Sundays. Sunday was family day for the Campbells; Dave got mad if we made other plans. Maybe next Saturday then, they said. Maybe we could get an earlier start, get the other wall done, and stand them both and tie them together. Sure, I said, and let Rodrigo drive me home.

He was drunk. I told him next week I'd drive myself over and asked him what time. Eight, he said. Nine, I figured. It had been altogether less entertaining than I had expected, not at all like back home. I didn't feel like I'd accomplished anything and I didn't feel like I'd made a new friend. I'd gotten the impression the other day that Rodrigo was a laid-back, relaxed sort of guy, who liked to take things slow and easy—like Cipi. Fact is, he was stoned. He'd had at least a six-pack for himself that day, not to mention I don't know how many joints he snuck off and smoked while everyone else was working. I wondered if Diana's grandmother knew about that. Anyway, I figured I might as well go back again next week. I had nothing better to do.

It was full dark when he dropped me off in front of Dave's house. The front porch light was on and Dave was outlined against the windows that flanked the front door. Waiting up. If Dad ever waited up, he did it unobtrusively: reading in his bed upstairs. Standing by the window, I thought, was rude. He opened the door just before I got to it.

"Who was that who dropped you off?" he asked, before I was even inside.

"That was Rodrigo, the guy I went to help with his garage today."

Dave looked out the window again, then switched off the light and followed me into the kitchen. I tossed my jacket on a chair and went to get a glass of water. That was another gripe I had about the city. The water. I was used to that famous Pure Rocky Mountain Spring Water. What I was drinking here was treated with chemicals because people dumped sewage into it. Delightful. And doctors wonder why there's so much cancer in the modern world.

"Where did you say you met this guy?" Dave asked. He was still hanging around, as if he had something on his mind.

"At school."

"He goes to your school?"

"He goes to the Catholic school, wherever that is. His cousin goes to my school. That's how we met, when I missed the bus."

"Two days ago?"

"Yeah."

"And today you spent the whole day out with him."

"Working. I spent the whole day with his entire family. Working. It's not like we were out cruising bars or something."

"What makes you mention bars?"

"Nothing."

His suspicion irritated me. I drank the water and put the glass in the dishwasher, and when I turned around, he was still standing there.

"Where was this garage you helped work on?"

"Uh. I don't know. Ninth, I think the street was. Something like that."

"Down near the railroad?"

"Yeah. Few blocks from there."

"You didn't mention that when you asked if you could go over there today," Dave said.

"I didn't know where he lived till I went there."

"Will, I don't think I like you associating with this . . . Rodrigo, did you say his name is?"

"Yeah. And where do you come off telling me who to associate with when you never met the guy and don't even know his name yet?"

"Don't take that tone with me," he said. "I only meant that there are better neighborhoods than that . . ."

"Whiter ones too," I said.

"Where do you get that?"

"If his name was Roderick instead of Rodrigo, if he drove a new Toyota instead of that old piece of junk he can afford, you wouldn't have any problem with him."

"It's not his name I have a problem with, it's his neighborhood."

"Yeah. The wrong end of town, right? Where there's more Hispanics, Indians, Blacks..."

"No. I meant where there's more crime, drugs, and undesirable characters. Why are you trying to twist things before I even get a chance to say them?"

"Maybe to save you the trouble."

"Why did you mention bars today?" Dave said again. His nose wrinkled slightly, and I knew I smelled of marijuana smoke, cigarette smoke, and beer, even though I hadn't been using any of them myself. *Thanks a lot, Rodrigo,* I thought.

"Because you seem to expect it," I said. I left the kitchen and headed for the stairs.

"Will!" he hollered after me.

"Billy!" I shouted back, and slammed the bathroom door. I started undressing for a shower, and stopped suddenly. Stupid, I thought, getting into a fight with Dave when it was Rodrigo I was mad at. Rodrigo, or myself even. I'd expected to go out to a neighborhood where people spoke Spanish, and find a lifestyle like the one I'd left a thousand miles away. This was a city, not a little mountain village. Mr. Montaño was not a substitute for John Henry Gonzales. Or Sal Delgado. Or Dad. I left the water running to warm up, but I opened the door and started to go downstairs and apologize to Dave. I got as far as the top of the steps though, and heard him talking to Mom.

"There are hundreds of decent kids in that school, so why is it after just a few days, he ties up with some kid from down by the river and comes home smelling of beer and dope? I feel I've been patient with him, but I'm going to have to start laying down the law. This sort of behavior can't be tolerated. I know he's been through a hard time, but this has got to stop . . . here . . . now."

I went back upstairs, the anger creeping back. *He didn't even ask,* I thought. *Dammit, he didn't even ask!*

TEN

Monday I checked the mail for a letter from Dana. What I found was a letter from Cip.

> *Coyote,*
> *There's a lot of things I'd like to tell you about, what's going on at your place, all that. But first thing I have to tell you is that Rex is dead. Your dad told me he hadn't seen him around for a few days, and I'd heard of some trouble the ranchers were having down at the pastures near the river, so I went and*

looked and I found him there. They'd shot him. I don't suppose after hearing that you'd be real interested in hearing just gossip, so I'll write again in a couple days. I saw Charlie Silva, and your stuff's on its way. Man, I wish you hadn't gone.

Your Friend,
Cipriano Delgado

"What's the matter?" Cecilia asked. We'd been having an after-school snack in the kitchen while I read it. First letter I'd gotten from home, and it had to be like that.

"Someone shot my dog," I said.

"Are you serious?"

"Yeah." I wadded up the letter and tossed it in the garbage. She thought I was making a sick joke, I guess. She got the letter out and read it herself

"That's awful! People can't just go around shooting dogs. This Charlie Silva guy's a sheriff or something isn't he? Maybe you should write to him and have him arrest them."

"If he was bothering cows, he got what he deserved," I said.

"Billy!"

"Look, Cecil, I know a lot of people think cattle ranchers are rich, but most people who run cows in our mountains have herds of anything from two to fifteen cows, seldom any more. You lose one calf to a dog pack, and it could mean a loss of up to fifty percent of your annual income. That's not acceptable. Dogs who kill livestock get shot. I've shot a few of them myself."

"But this was your dog!"

"He apparently didn't learn as well as I thought he did," I said, and I went upstairs to my room.

It was all true, what I told Cecilia, but it still hurt to think Rex was dead. He was big and ugly, but he was good-natured and gentle—most of the time. What a lot of people don't understand about dogs is that they're more dangerous than wolves. Dogs that run loose seem to naturally form packs, and dogs don't fear humans the way wolves do. Sometimes the packs kill for food, but sometimes, warped by city living and easy food, they kill without need. Sort of like human sport hunters.

Rex had been part of a dog pack when he was a pup, one that had been harassing cows in the Spring Mountain area for months. When spring came up and the calves were dropping, Cipi, Bobby, and I went on horseback and camped for several days to guard their dads' cattle and look out for the pack. We caught them slaughtering a calf in the moonlight. The way they ripped and shredded a living animal they had no intention of eating was sickening, and I felt no remorse at all that my bullets hit two of them. We dropped four of the dogs, and the fifth, a half-grown pup, had a shattered bone in his hind leg that would never heal. That was Rex. I took him home, and everyone agreed that the fear and pain from being shot would likely break him of his pack-habits. For two years, he'd been a good pet. But if he was out there on the meadows where the cows were with a bullet in him now, he must have gone back to his old ways. If I'd been home, I might have had to shoot him myself, I thought. I was almost glad, for a moment, that I wasn't home.

After staring at the ceiling for almost half an hour, I got up and wrote back to Cip. I thanked him for the news, asked after Dad and Dana, and then got down to what I really wanted. Would he look around, please, to see if anyone had any snapshots with Rex in them? Maybe from last Fourth of July, the picnic on the river, or from the camping trip we'd taken in August. It was strange to have almost six years of life suddenly ripped away, without anything at all to remember them by but the pictures I carried in my own head. Worse than just strange, actually, since this was the second time it had happened to me.

Wednesday, when I got home from school, four boxes were waiting for me in the living room. Cecilia was so excited you'd have thought it was Christmas. Cecilia, I recalled, had always liked packages. She even liked ripping open stuff that she'd ordered and paid for in advance. She headed straight for the kitchen to get a knife to rip the strapping tape off, but I said, "I'll get them later. I have homework now," and I went upstairs to my bedroom.

I didn't have homework. I hardly ever brought schoolwork home, because I had all those study halls to do it in school. What I had was a sudden attack of something like stage fright. I didn't want to open those boxes. It seemed silly, after all that wait, but suddenly, I just didn't want to.

There was nothing easier the second time around about having my whole life ripped out of my hands. But maybe everyone here was right about wanting me to get new things, to replace the old. Everything in those boxes was going to be a reminder of what I couldn't get through the mail. Every shirt would be a shirt I wore when I was with Dana, or the guys. Every pair of jeans, every personal item, was going to remind me of Dad or Rex or something that I'd never see again. Maybe I'd be better off not opening them, ever.

I delayed, anyway, till after supper, when everyone gathered in the living room to watch. I was out of excuses. I took the knife Cecilia offered me and slit open the smallest of the boxes.

Nothing inside attacked. It was just clothes. Shirts, jeans, work boots, stuff like that. Cecilia went through it all carefully, making unfriendly comments on my taste in clothes. The next box was my winter coat, some camping stuff, record albums, cassette tapes, books, an old rodeo poster, and other odds and ends. That bothered me, because I didn't own all that much stuff, and I couldn't figure out why there were two more boxes left unopened. I stood there studying them, as if the shape could give me a clue as to what was inside, while Cecilia went through all my clothes and tapes. When she'd satisfied her curiosity about those things, she was ready to see what was in the next box. When she started pestering too much, I cut the tape on the biggest, heaviest box.

Inside were two bright-colored Mexican blankets, a hat rack made from a section sliced off a cedar tree, peeled and polished. A saddle pad and blanket. A pair of chaps. A pair of spurs. My lassos and pigging ropes. My stopwatch. And my saddle.

They were admiring the hat rack—which I had made. They were examining the bright, cheap ragcotton blankets. No one noticed the saddle till I drew it out of the box and lugged it over to drop it on the arm of the sofa. I draped the spurs around the saddle horn and stood there looking at it, wondering what in the world I was going to do with a saddle in the city.

"What is that?" Dave asked.

"It's a saddle," I said.

"Duh," Cecilia said.

Dave came over and ran a hand across the rope-patterned leather stretched over the curve of the cantle. "What a waste of money and effort," he said.

"What?" I said. "I think it looks nice."

"I meant sending it here. It couldn't have been easy to pack or cheap to send, but here it sits." He sighed, and shook his head. "What a cruel thing to do."

"What's cruel?"

"Sending you this. I can only assume it was meant to remind you of all the fun you had playing cowboy."

"I didn't play cowboy," I said. "I was a cowboy. *Am* a cowboy! He sent me this because it belongs to me!"

"And what are you going to do with it now that it's here? Use it for a car seat? We can't exactly keep a horse in the back yard, you know. The wise thing would have been just to keep it in New Mexico."

"Dad has a saddle," I said, looking down and stroking the soft fawn-colored leather. "Mr. Melendez, I mean. He has two, in fact. He doesn't need this. He didn't send it to me to remind me of old times. He sent it because it's mine."

"Yes. And it has absolutely no value to you here

and now, which means he could only have sent it to influence your thinking and possibly pressure you into running off to the rodeo instead of going on to college..."

"And throwing my life away?" I demanded. "Like he did?"

"I didn't say..."

"Yeah? Where else could you have gone with that? Well, maybe my dad didn't end up in some fancy big city with a giant house too big for his family and two cars, but that doesn't mean he threw his life away either! There's more to life than big incomes, you know!"

"I know. And this attitude of yours is exactly what I was talking about before you interrupted me."

"What attitude?"

"The one where you are yelling at me about a lifestyle I have said nothing at all against, in defense of the fact that, useful or not, there's a saddle sitting here in the living room. You don't need it, I can't imagine that you even thought of asking for it on your own, but you're standing there ready to fight for it and all it can represent. I'm sure if you think about it you can see why I consider sending this saddle to be a manipulative move."

"I can think about that. Can you think about this? Maybe it *was* sent out of generosity. Dad's not a monster."

“That’s a matter of opinion,” Dave muttered.

I could understand his feelings, really, but the fact that he said that made me mad. I grabbed the saddle and lifted it to the back of the sofa and slammed it down hard. A western saddle like that weighs a lot. It can slam good.

“*Value,* huh? You want to talk about *value.* That was the word you used a minute ago, right? The thing has no *value* here. So let’s talk about *value.* The value of this thing is enough to pay for maybe a whole year of your precious college. Is that enough *value* for you?”

“It’s a saddle, Will. Not a job.”

“That’s right. It’s a saddle. A custom-designed, hand-made work of art. Look at it! Special carving on the skirts and trapaderos, carving on the fork, silver conchos all over it, rope-patterned cantle. Two, three thousand dollars, easy, even after the light use it’s had! An old man had this special made for his grandson. After the kid graduated high school, they were going into the rodeo together as team ropers. But the kid was killed by a drunk driver on graduation night. The old man knew Dad and me, knew I had an interest in roping, and he gave the saddle to me. *Gave* it to me. But you don’t want me to have it anymore. It doesn’t fit your image of what I should be. So let’s just get rid of it, right . . . ?”

“Will . . .”

"Will. Yeah. Don't you understand, I don't like that name? I never liked it. Everyone calls me 'Billy' now, 'Billy' is what I answer to, but 'Billy' doesn't fit your image of me either. So let's throw that out too. Let's just throw out everything that doesn't fit your image of what you thought I should be when you came to kidnap me back."

"Will, you're overreacting."

"I'm overreacting? You make a big case about how Dad is trying to control my life just because I got a few of my own belongings back and you think I'm overreacting?"

"You're shouting."

"I'm pissed! You want to get rid of the saddle. Fine. We'll do what you want. My name has to go. Well, you're the boss, right?"

"Will..."

"What's next? My clothes maybe aren't good enough? Do I read the wrong books? Listen to the wrong music? You don't have to worry about making me get rid of my dog, you saw to that already when I had to abandon him and someone shot him for you..."

"William James Campbell!"

"What?"

Dave took a deep breath and stopped shouting. "I'm sorry about your dog. And I'm sorry about the comment I made about Mr. Melendez. That wasn't fair.

You may keep the saddle. You're right. It's yours."

I didn't answer right away. I just looked at it and thought, *What am I going to do with it, anyway?*

"Will?"

"I'm sorry. I got a little wild, too."

"It's a lovely saddle," Mom said. "And with the history it has, you should be proud of it."

"I am."

Dave and I looked at each other, but I looked away. I didn't want to look him in the eye. There was too much understanding in his look, and I was still mad.

"Well. Shall we open the last box?" he said, almost managing to sound normal.

"It can wait," I said. Instead, I shoved my clothes back into their boxes for carrying upstairs.

I'd had this sudden bizarre thought that I hadn't done much roping before I got that saddle. Like, what if Dave was right, that owning something like that puts ideas into your head? But that was stupid, really. Dave was the one that put that idea in my mind and it bothered me that I'd let him. I hadn't done much roping before I got it because I got it years ago when I could hardly ride. I *liked* roping, and I'd have learned it and worked at it on that fancy saddle, or on the old beat-up one that had been in Dad's family since his grandfather was a kid.

Besides, I didn't want to open the last box. I had

figured out what was in it. All my stuff was already open and scattered around. There was only one other thing I owned — besides my truck, and that didn't fit in a box that size — and if the saddle was going to cause a fight, I didn't want to know what that last thing would start.

"Come on, Will," Cecilia said, ignoring the argument and picking at the packing tape. I didn't use the kitchen knife on this one. I opened the leather knife case I found under my saddle and snapped open a folding Buck knife, locking the blade carefully into place. My knife. I used to carry it almost everywhere. I didn't carry a knife because I thought I was tough. I carried one for survival. A knife and a fistful of matches can get you through an amazing lot of things if you get lost in the mountains, or thrown by a horse. You don't carry folding knives in the city, though. In the city, knives aren't for surviving. They're for hurting. I looked at this one. It was pretty, with a bear etched in the bone handle, but long and razor sharp, too. Useless as the saddle. Well, not quite. Knives were good for chores and carpentry, too.

"How come this one says it's from someone else?" Cecilia asked. "The return address says Ben Jar-something, not Charlie Silva."

"Jaramillo," I said. Ben Jaramillo was a local outfitter. He bought and sold so many guns in his business that he was a licensed gun merchant. Only a licensed gun merchant can ship firearms. That's another reason I knew what was inside the box. Oh well. They were all waiting. I slit open the tape and pulled out the packing.

It was packed in a Styrofoam holder that was carved out in the middle so the rifle was set right down inside it, and was wrapped around with strapping tape to keep it from slipping out of the Styrofoam. Cecilia stared down into the box, and breathed, "Oh, Billy!"

"Do you have any nail polish remover?" I asked her.

"Huh? Uh, yeah."

"Could I use some?"

"On what? What is it?" Dave asked.

"To clean the sticky tape residue off," I said. I slit the tape holding the rifle in place and lifted it carefully out of the box, keeping the muzzle pointed straight up at the ceiling. No way it was loaded. The clip for the bullets and the bolt had both been removed and were in separate little niches in the Styrofoam. Still, I ran a finger in where the bolt goes to make sure a round wasn't stuck up in there, and made sure the safety was on. In those gun safety lessons that the Game & Fish Department gives, the biggest lesson they drilled home was treat every firearm as if it was loaded. Never assume it isn't, even if it came from someone as trustworthy as Ben Jaramillo.

"'I didn't know it was loaded' is about the stupidest thing a person can say," Dad told me years back. "And the deadliest."

"Oh, my God," Dave said.

It was a nice gun. A Winchester bolt-action .30-30 with both a small three-power flip-scope and open sights. The stock was walnut and had some basket-weave carving on it. This was the gun I hunted stray dogs with. Also bear once (kind of accidentally), deer annually, and elk last winter.

"Will," Dave started hesitantly.

"I already know," I said. "I know how you feel about guns. Let me clean the tape-smears off it so it doesn't end up with rust or anything, and I'll pack it away."

"Can't we just send it back?" Mom asked.

"We can't mark it refused, because it's already been opened, and only a licensed gun dealer can ship fire-arms."

"Can you sell it?" Cecilia asked. She was back already with the nail polish remover, and I accepted a little cotton-ball full and rubbed it on the barrel where it was sticky.

"Will?" Dave said. They were all so edgy, like I was going to start shooting everybody in sight, or drop it and kill myself. I don't think anyone but me had taken a normal breath since I pulled it out.

"I'd rather not sell it, if I have a choice," I said. I got the stickiness off the barrel and laid the gun back into its niche. There was no tape on the clip, but Ben had taped down the bolt, carefully taping only the handle, not the part that had to slide into the gun. Still, I pulled that out and cleaned it too.

"You can't use it in the city."

"It's not like I ran around with a loaded rifle all the time in the country either," I said. "We kept our rifles locked up almost all year, took them out every November for the deer hunt, and except for the time the dogs were killing calves, that was it."

"You shot Bambi," Cecilia said, wrinkling her nose.

"No," I said. "Any deer that talked we shipped off to Barnum and Bailey."

"You know what I mean. How could you kill a deer? They're so sweet."

"They are actually," I said. "Almost like pork. I prefer elk meat to deer meat, but I'll eat whatever I can get."

"Ugh!" Cecilia said. "You sure grew up gross!"

"I don't approve of hunting," Dave said.

"A lot of people don't approve of hunting," Dad told me, that first year we went up together. "There's a lot of criminals in the woods with guns who call themselves hunters, a lot of people who consider it a sport, too. Killing for sport and shooting up everything in sight

gives hunters a bad name, but to me, it's something different. To hunt you have to feel the forest, breathe it, and live it. You have to learn to recognize tracks and animal habits, you have to move through these woods as if you were an animal yourself, not just a tourist. Besides, it's a family tradition. Men in our family have been hunting meat for the table right here in these mountains since the days they did their hunting with bows and arrows. Right up to when I went into the rodeo, I was supplying the family through the winter with what I killed in the woods. A couple deer or an elk will still see the two of us through a whole year."

I was supposed to go hunting with Cody, Cip, and Bobby this year. I held the gun in my hands again and I could smell ponderosa needles breaking underfoot, I could smell dried leaves and seasoned grass, and the dampness of the creek bottoms. I could feel the chill air of a high-country early winter, feel the touch of snow against my cheek as it fell, muffling footsteps through the undergrowth. I was not going to sell this gun.

"I do approve of hunting," I said.

"Will . . ."

"I'll pack it up. I'll even put it up in the attic. No one will ever know it's there."

"I'll know it's there."

"For God's sake, I don't even have any bullets!"

"Please!" Mom said. "We'll discuss it later. Can you put it in the attic for now?"

"I'll take it," Dave said.

"I know how to handle a firearm," I said. Why did he think that Dad would give a gun to someone too ignorant to handle it safely? I knew more what I was doing than Dave did. I don't think he had even seen a gun close up before. I'd handled them for years now, took the course, went hunting. I could put away a rifle.

I put everything back in the box and packed the paper down over it tight, folded the top flaps in.

We didn't yell anymore. But I heard Dave expressing what he had wanted to say to me later that night to Mom. Their door was shut and his tone was fairly low, but words like "Accident" and "Kill" and "Maimed" came out into the hall, and I thought again, *How stupid does he think I am?*

ELEVEN

"Hi!"

I was sitting in the student center during afternoon study hall, when Diana Rodriguez sat down across the table from me.

"Hi," I said back.

"Working on math, huh?"

"Yeah."

"I just did mine. You got study hall this hour every day? Of course you do, what a stupid question. You're a junior, right? If this was your PE study hall, you'd be in PE today. It's Thursday."

"Yeah."

"I have PE this period, but I'm a sophomore, so it's Monday, Wednesday, and Friday. I've seen you in here before, actually, but I never came up and talked to you before, because I never knew you before. So. How's life?"

"I'd rather not think about it."

"That bad, huh? Heard from your girlfriend yet?"

"No."

"Well, I wouldn't worry about it. Probably she's a lot like me. Loves to get letters, hates to write them. I heard from my boyfriend today."

"I didn't know you had one. Is he in another town somewhere, too?"

"Nope," she said. "Lives right here. Goes to this school and everything. Convenient, huh?"

"Yeah. That's nice."

"Yeah. Saw him today, right here in the student center before class. He had a special message for me. Want to guess what it is?"

"I really have no idea."

"He came in here to tell me that he was taking Heather Rhodes to the dance tomorrow night. The big Halloween Costume Dance in the gym. I'm sure you've seen the posters."

"Yeah. Uh, why is your boyfriend taking some other girl to the dance?"

"Gee. I don't know. You think maybe it's his way of telling me he won't be taking me to that dance?"

I looked up sharply and saw that despite her cheery smile and easy chatter, her eyes didn't look quite as sparkly as they had the other day. It could have been the lighting, I suppose. But then again, maybe not.

"I'm sorry," I said, meaning it.

"Yeah, well. It wasn't exactly the romance of the century, you know? We've only been seeing each other about a month. He was the first guy that ever asked me out."

"Well, I'm sure he won't be the last."

"You kidding? With the kind of rumors he's started spreading about me already I should get lots of offers. Thanks, anyway," she added with a touch of bitterness. Then, out of nowhere, she said, "You and your Dana ever sleep together?"

"That's none of your business," I said.

"I'm taking a poll," she said, and pulled out a blank piece of paper as if she was serious. "I want to know if it's true that nobody in this modern age hangs on to their virginity all the way up to their sixteenth birthday. Actually," she added, putting the paper down again. "I don't hold virginity as such a great treasure, and I don't intend to run off and become a nun right after graduation. The thing is, though, that fifteen isn't all that old, and I have enough problems right now without trying to juggle a sex life in with the rest of it. You know?"

"No."

"You don't know?"

"I was answering your first question. I never slept with Dana."

"Anyone else?"

"Dana was the first girl I ever cared enough for that I wanted to do it with her out of desire for the person, not desire for the act, if that makes sense."

"It does. What stopped you? Or wasn't she ready?"

"I don't know if she was or not. The opportunity just never came up."

"Well, if the opportunity did come up, I mean, a real sincere opportunity, like all of her family goes to California without her for a week and asks you to house-sit, and she said she wasn't ready for that sort of commitment, what would you do?"

"Why do you put it like that? Do I look like a rapist to you?"

"No, I don't mean like that. I mean, would you talk her into it?"

"No. Dana means too much to me. Getting someone to do something they don't want to do can hurt them. I wouldn't hurt her for anything. But, are you hinting that your boyfriend broke up with you because you wouldn't go to bed with him?"

"It's probably more complicated than that. I hope it's more complicated than that! It seems to be a key issue, though."

"He sounds like a real jerk then. If you don't mind my saying so."

"Why should I mind? He *is* a jerk."

"I got that impression. But sometimes, when a girl's mad at a guy and tells you bad things about him, and you call him a jerk to be sympathetic, she'll knock your teeth out in his defense. Girls can be very strange," I added, then realized who I was talking to. "Sorry."

"No need to apologize," she grinned at me. "I agree."

"So. Are you . . . okay?"

"I don't know. I'm mostly mad right now. Maybe I'll hurt tomorrow. Partly it's this dance thing. I mean, we planned on going to this since they announced it. I spent two weeks making a costume. And then, he pulls this crap the day before the dance. I mean, I know he did it to make fun of me. All his friends will be there, they'll all be sitting around with him and his new chick, laughing at me. I'd really like to go to that stupid dance and show him up. But..."

"Yeah?"

"Well, if I go stag, I'm still an object of pity, right? They can laugh at me or feel sorry for me, but I'm there in all my feathers and beads alone, and there he is with Heather, who is disgustingly gorgeous and has a reputation that would curl your hair. Which is really why I came over here to talk to you."

"You want me to give you a reputation to match hers?"

She laughed. "No! See, I thought all day about how bad I still want to go to that dance, but like I said, I can't go alone. That won't prove anything. What I really wanted was to sort of flaunt it in front of him, show him how bad I don't need him, you know? So, I thought maybe I could get Rodrigo to take me. He's easy to talk into things like that. He'll do anything, because he doesn't care about anything. But he's my cousin, and everybody knows it, because there's very few Hispanics in this part of town, so we sort of stick out. And going to a dance with your cousin is as much a pity-thing as going alone. So then I saw you sitting here, and remembered that you're nice and easy to talk to and your girlfriend is a thousand miles away, so maybe I could ask you to take me to the dance."

"You want me...?"

"It wouldn't be like a real date or anything. I understand about this Dana of yours, and I'm not trying to put the moves on you. It would just be a favor for an old friend—a new friend," she amended, grinning again. I just want Jack and everybody else to know I don't need him, and him dumping me like that is nothing to me. I want *revenge."*

"It sounds to me like you deserve it," I said. "Sure, I'll go to the dance with you."

"Great! And look, I invited you, so I'll take care of everything—tickets, transportation, you don't have to do anything at all."

"No, that won't work. You buy the tickets and people will think you had to buy a date, then it won't be much of a revenge. I'll take care of it all."

"Who would know?" she asked.

"I don't know. But people talk. Don't worry about it. I'll even pick up the tickets today instead of buying them at the door, and probably I can get the car for Friday night."

"Just probably? Your folks don't trust you to borrow the car?"

"I don't know. I've only been living with them for two weeks. I never asked for the car before."

"Oh, yeah. Custody suits or something."

"Yeah. But, I'm a pretty good driver. I don't see why they wouldn't let me."

"If they don't, let me know, and I'll get Rodrigo to drive us. My grandma always tried to get him to drive on my dates with Jack, so I'd have a chaperon, but Jack got his license two weeks ago, and that put an end to that. Pretty much put an end to our relationship too, come to think of it. Well"—she stood up, gathering her books—"this is gonna be fun. Thanks."

"Hey! I need your address, and probably directions to find it too. I don't know this town real well."

"Yeah. Right," she laughed, and bent over to write it down on a piece of paper she tore out of my notebook: a house number and a map.

"Okay. We're all set then," I said, and she waved and hurried off, because the bell had rung while she was writing down her address. I looked down at the paper and thought about it. She was a nice kid. It sounded to me like this Jack guy had treated her bad, and I figured she deserved her night at the dance, for whatever good that was going to do anybody. If Dana was here, no way she'd understand. Of course, if Dana was here, I'd be taking her to the dance. I folded up the paper, tucked it into my math book, and went to seventh period.

"Mom," I said that afternoon after school, "do you think I could use the car tomorrow night to take a girl to the Halloween dance at school?"

"You're going to the dance?" she asked, smiling at me.

"Yeah."

"That's great, honey! I don't see any reason why you can't use the car for a date, as long as you follow all the rules. But you know that. Oh, I'm so glad you're starting to make friends," she added, brushing at my hair with her hand. "Do you need help with a costume?"

I hadn't given it a thought, really, but I just shrugged and said, "I'll think of something."

In the end, I went as a cowboy. I know: that's too easy. But dress-up things make me feel silly. Cecilia really got into it, though. She was Dracula's Daughter with her red hair in ringlets down her back, and a flowing white thing like a nightgown for a dress. She had talon-length blood red fingernails and blood red lipstick and had rubbed some kind of white stuff on her face to make her look dead. Very effective. Her date was picking her up at the house. I had the keys to the Karmann Ghia in my pocket.

"Thanks," I said to Dave, about the keys.

"Take care of it," was all he said back. Then, "Who is this girl you're going out with? Do we know her?"

"Not likely, as many kids as there are in that school," Cecilia answered for me.

"Her name's Diana," I said.

"You must mean Diana Cuthbertson," Cecilia said. "She's in our homeroom. Man, do you move in high circles."

I opened my mouth to say I didn't mean Diana Cuthbertson, I didn't even know who she was, but Dave was already asking, "Why do you say that, Cecil? Who is she?"

"Who isn't she? She's vice-president of the Student Council, Drama Club, French Club, homecoming princess. She lives way out west of here, one of those huge houses with the big yards and tall fences around them, you know? I understand her father's a psychiatrist, and her poor mother's just a plain old everyday M.D."

They looked so pleased, I hated to correct them, so I just didn't say anything.

"Have fun, both of you," Dave said, and after he snapped a few photographs, I got in the car and went to find Diana's house. I still wasn't used to the car. I'd driven stick shifts before, but it had always been trucks. A work truck like mine has four speeds, but they're compound, first, second, and third. You don't use compound, which is in the standard first-gear position, for anything but steep hills and heavy loads. I had to get out of the habit of skipping it in the Ghia, and I kept losing reverse, since where I thought it should be was fifth gear on the little high-geared car.

Diana didn't live in the same neighborhood as Rodrigo. Her directions took me to the other side of the railroad tracks and across a river. All the houses there—except one that had been repainted since spring—had muddy high-water marks about three feet up from the ground.

Diana's address marked a tall, gabled house that was covered in faded siding. It sat a couple feet up off the ground, and windows peeking out of the foundation indicated it had a basement, though what good a basement was in view of those high-water marks, I didn't know. There was a garage at the side that looked like it probably wasn't used much, as there was a '52 Pontiac rusting away on blocks in front of the closed door.

The front door of the house was wood with a long oval window set in it. I went up and knocked. In a moment, a figure appeared through the hazy curtain over the glass and the door opened, leaving me still on the far side of a screen door.

"Yes?"

I assumed this was the grandmother. She was a tiny little woman with gray hair, a lot of wrinkles, and very sharp black eyes.

"I'm Billy Campbell," I told her in Spanish. "I've come to take Diana to the dance."

Her lips twitched once, like she was trying to hide

some emotion or other. She pushed open the screen door and stepped back so I could enter the house.

"Diana is almost ready. I am her grandmother," she said, also in Spanish, when I was inside. A test maybe, to see if I'd memorized certain lines or could actually speak the language. I told her I was pleased to meet her, and her lips made another twitch as she studied me.

"Billy?" Diana's voice floated down from upstairs. "I'll be right down."

I didn't feel comfortable shouting back, so I didn't. I just stood there inside the door, looking around. Every time I looked toward the grandmother, I found her staring at me, and it made me nervous, so I didn't look at her much.

The front door opened directly into a living room that had faded rose wallpaper with mud and water stains along the base. There were stacks of magazines on the coffee table, women's magazines about crochet patterns and cookie recipes mostly, and a whole gallery of photographs on the end table under the lamp. Among other faces in the mass, I picked out an old school portrait of Diana, and a picture of a wellbrushed boy that could have been Rodrigo about ten years ago.

"Okay. Here I come!" Diana announced, and she came down the steps. "What do you think?"

I didn't answer, because I didn't think at all at first, I just stared. It was incredible.

Her costume consisted of a dress that was no more than a narrow cylinder of silky gold material that started under her arms and ended above her knees. It had strings to hold it over her shoulders, and was covered top to bottom with row after row of gold fringe. There were black velvet bows tied under her knees to look like garters, and she had on some antique-looking shoes and a feather boa.

"Think it came out all right?" she asked, turning in front of me. "I'm supposed to be a flapper." Without her usual baggy men's clothes, she was slender and delicate looking, and the dark gold of the costume brought out rich gold tones in her pale skin and gold highlights in her copper hair.

"I wanted blue or something," she said. "But I also wanted fringe, and all the fabric store had was red, black, and gold fringe. I don't like black, and with my hair I can't wear red, so all that left was gold."

"But the gold suits her, don't you think?" Grandma asked, in perfect English this time.

"Yeah," I said.

"Grandma!" Diana said.

"No. I mean it. I was about to mention that myself. That looks great. You really made it yourself?"

"Yeah. Well, I got the idea when we found the shoes and boa at a garage sale." She looked me over and shook her head sadly. "No imagination. Think anyone will recognize you?" I had on my usual clothes, a hat and spurs, and had my rope over one shoulder.

I opened my mouth to answer but she said, "I was kidding! It looks good. Really. Well. Shall we go?"

"Yeah," I said, and I held the door for her, which seemed to be the right thing to do in her grandmother's eyes. "Goodbye, Mrs. Rodriguez," I said. "Pleased to meet you."

"Eleven o'clock," she said.

"Yes, ma'am."

"Sharp."

"Yes, ma'am."

I walked with Diana out to where I'd parked the car at the curb, and unlocked her door.

"Wow. Fancy wheels. Your dad lets you drive this?"

"My uncle. And, yeah. I guess so. For tonight anyway."

She bent down and peeked inside, then straightened, turned, and hollered at the house, "It's okay, Grandma, I'll be safe with him. It has a stick shift between the seats in front and no back seat!"

The old woman, watching from the doorway, made a shooing-away gesture of mock irritation and shut the door. Laughing, Diana climbed down into the car. I went around and got in next to her.

"I don't think she has to worry much about you," I said. "I think you can take care of yourself. I think you already did take care of yourself."

"Yeah," she said, smiling in a self-satisfied way. I did, didn't I?"

The big gym had that soft floor on it, so the dance was in the small gym. They had decorated it with black and orange streamers and balloons, paper pumpkins and skeletons. There was a small, very loud band set up in one corner, and a couple long trestle tables with punch bowls and cookies near the entrance. I noticed that even though there were quite a few kids and costumes of every possible description, we got a few looks. Being with a girl pretty enough to turn heads is always a good feeling, even if she isn't really yours.

"That one," Diana said, pointing. You couldn't tell much about what the guy looked like though, with the gorilla mask on. I was surprised she could even recognize him.

"What do you think of Heather? Seriously, I mean. From a guy's point of view."

"That would be the blonde in the Sheena of the Jungle skirt?"

"Yeah. I suppose really she is prettier than I am. I mean, she looks just like Barbie, right? Same hair, same baby-face, same build."

"She doesn't hold a candle to you," I said.

"Man, what a gentleman!"

"I'm serious. Why is it you won't believe it when I compliment you?"

"Because the first time Grandma pressured you to say something nice, and now *I* did, asking for a comparison."

"Look at her eyes, Di. It's like you said. She looks like a Barbie doll, she even has plastic eyes. Your eyes are anything but plastic. They're so alive, they're scary. And anyway, I never cared much for blondes. They're too pale and washed-out looking. I like darker girls."

"Do you have a picture of your Dana?"

"My Dana. You always talk about her like she's a pet. Yeah. I got one." I pulled out my wallet and showed her the little school portrait of Dana I carried in there.

"Pretty," Diana said.

"Thanks," I said, putting it away.

"Look, Billy. I'm sorry."

"About what?"

"Tricking you into coming here. I mean, like I said, it's not really a date, but it wasn't fair, either, the way I told you my troubles first and then asked you. If you had refused, you'd have been a jerk, right? I figured you for the gentlemanly type, and I used it against you. That's why you've been sort of quiet all night, isn't it?"

"No. It isn't. I'm sorry I haven't been better company. I guess I just don't want to be here."

"We can leave," she said. She'd been so bright and sparkly when I picked her up. Now she looked like someone had turned the lights off from inside.

"No, Di. I'm sorry, I didn't mean that."

"You don't have to apologize for how you feel."

"Look. If I've been quiet tonight, it's because I've got a few things on my mind."

"Like this Dana you care so much about."

"Like that I don't want to be here. In this state, I meant. In this city. In this house. I just want to go home. But I can't; I don't seem to have any say in the matter at all. And since I have to be here . . . well, I'd rather be here at this dance with you than anywhere else in this lousy state."

"Like I said," she smiled. "A gentleman."

I ended up telling her everything. About Dad coming to the baseball practices in disguise, about the time on the rodeo circuit, about the accident and moving to Monte Verde, about the stupid mistake I'd made at the bar, and Dave. Everything. She listened, intent but without comment, till I was done.

"Strange," she said. "You sound kind of hostile about this Uncle Dave of yours, yet I would have thought you two got along all right."

"Why?"

"I don't know, exactly. But, he did let you use his sports car tonight, didn't he? There must be some trust or something there."

"There's some guilt there, is what there is. I owned my own truck in Monte Verde. I admit it's not next year's model, but I bought it myself, even put a new engine in it. Took me all summer to get it fixed up right so that when I got my license I'd have my own wheels, too. My truck is one of the casualties in this battle. Dave won't even talk about it, but I know he sold it. Every time I mention 'truck' he says we'll talk about it later, but he already had someone sell it for me back home."

"How do you know?"

"Mrs. C de Baca, she's the lady who does everything for the credit union back home. She's like a teller, loan officer, bookkeeper, everything. The credit union office is on her sun porch still. Anyway, she'll cut people a lot of slack about getting into accounts of sons and husbands and whatever, because she knows everybody in town, but she wouldn't transfer my whole account here without my signature on it. So, she sent me a letter and an account transfer certificate, and my account is more than three thousand dollars above what it should be."

"Three . . . ?"

"Yeah. So. They got a good price for the truck, but I didn't hear anyone asking me about it. I figure the main reason Dave let me have the car tonight is guilt."

"Well. I guess it's between you and him anyway. Whatever happens, I don't really know either of you well enough to comment on it. But, I wish you luck."

"Thanks," I said. "And now I have to apologize. I brought you to this dance, and all we've done, almost, is sit back here and talk about my problems. You want to dance?"

"Sure!"

We danced a couple times, got some cookies and punch, danced some more. I'd assumed, cheerful and talkative as she was, that Diana would have a lot of friends at school, but she hardly seemed to know anyone. A few people said hi to her, and she made it a point to go over and say hello to her ex-boyfriend and his date, but other than that, we were alone most of the night. I sure didn't know anyone. But, I kind of liked it. I enjoyed her company. She went back to being sparkly. Generally, she was pretty fun to be around, and I didn't really feel like meeting a bunch of new people just then anyway. At ten-thirty we left the dance and I drove her home.

"I had a good time," she said in the car.

"You sound surprised."

"I was thinking it was going to be like a war or something. I just went to show off for Jack and Heather, but I enjoyed being with you a lot more than seeing him there. I hope you don't mind I said that."

"No. Why would I?"

"Because of Dana."

I wanted to say to her that though I liked her a lot, I didn't feel about her like I felt about Dana. I felt more like I feel about Cecilia. If I had a younger sister, instead of an older one, I'd like to have one like her. I was afraid, though, that if I said that, I might phrase it wrong and hurt her feelings. Instead I said, "We can be friends, can't we?"

That seemed to please her. "Yeah. Why not? You realize though, that I'm going to have to do something to pay you back. Take you to a movie or something."

"You don't have to."

"No. Really. There must be something you'd like to do that you couldn't do alone."

"Well, I love a good *rancheras* two-step. That's my kind of dancing, not this stuff where you move around and never touch your partner."

"No kidding?"

"No kidding. I'm a lot better at it, too."

"I should hope so. You're not much of a modern dancer."

"Thanks so much. Anyway, I doubt that anyone out here even knows what *rancheras* is."

"Sure, I know. It's like country and western, only Spanish style, right? The band my cousin is hiring for her wedding plays a lot of that junk and nobody but a couple old men got the slightest idea of how to dance to it. Hey, that's it!"

"What's it?"

"I'll take you to my cousin's wedding."

"I don't know your cousin."

"That's okay. She's having such a big wedding, she won't even know half the people there herself. She has twelve bridesmaids lined up. I'm one of them."

"Then you'll have a date, whoever it is you stand up with at the wedding."

"Theoretically, right. But she has me standing up with her fiancé's cousin who I don't even know, and he's bringing his girlfriend. So, why shouldn't I bring along my own dancing partner, too? It's in November, a week before Thanksgiving. Although why anyone in their right mind gets married in November, I don't know. She's having us all dress up in spring colors, too. Lavender and peach and lime and rose, for crying out loud. If you have to get married in November, you should wear rust and gold velvet, not rose tulle."

"Right," I said, though I had no idea what she was talking about.

"Anyway, you want to come?"

"I guess I could. It sounds like fun."

"Okay. It's a date then. Ooops! I mean, it's a plan. This Dana, is she the jealous type?"

"Extremely."

"Well, then. I'm real glad she's a thousand miles away!"

We got to her house a little before eleven, and the porch light was on. Grandma stood behind the filmy front door curtain and watched while I helped Diana out of the car and walked her to the door. Somehow, it didn't seem as rude having a grandmother wait up for a fifteen-year-old girl after a dance as it had seemed when Dave was standing there watching me come home at dusk from visiting friends. We said good night on the top step of the porch. It never occurred to me to kiss her good night; she just wasn't that sort of friend. But I wouldn't have anyway. Her grandma had opened the door and stood there waiting behind the screen door as we were coming up the front steps.

TWELVE

My curfew for the dance was twelve-thirty. I was early, and didn't feel much like going home anyway, so after I dropped Diana off, I took off and headed south out of town. There was no place in particular I intended to go, and I figured eventually I'd just turn around and go home. Mostly, I was interested in being alone. I hadn't been alone, really alone, since that night at the Mountain View Bar.

I let daydreams flick across my mind as I drove. I could imagine cruising like this all night. Dark, unlit highway, the moon hanging low overhead, the hum of the car's engine and the whine of the tires on the pavement. Me and the dark and the silence, and in the morning, I'd be where I could see mountains again. I-25, man, Denver to Raton, with the high peaks of the Rockies on your right all the way south. Take off before Raton maybe, wind slowly through one of those northern mountain passes, come in through Taos, Española, Santa Fe. Home.

Suddenly I was furious. It washed over me so unexpectedly my hands started shaking on the wheel and I pulled off the road into the parking lot of a big store that had appeared almost out of nowhere, the expanding outer edge of a small town a short way down the highway. I stopped the car in the deserted lot, killed the lights, turned off the engine and just sat there in the dark, feeling mad enough to kill someone, only for no reason at all.

No reason? Try three years of saving and searching for a truck that had four-wheel drive, was in decent shape and still wasn't too expensive. Try smashing fingers, bruising hands, skinning knuckles, and working in blistering heat in a stuffy, unventilated garage for two days pulling the blown engine out of that truck and replacing it with a nice, rebuilt Chevy 350, not to mention the free labor I'd traded to John Henry Gonzales in exchange for his help and the use of his garage. All gone. Oh, sure, I got some of the money back, but the labor, the time, and effort, that was gone.

"That we'll talk about later," Dave had said. But he didn't talk about it with me. He made up his mind and made his arrangements.

At least Dad had the courtesy to admit he was kidnapping me when he came and yanked my whole life out from under me. Dave kept trying to pretend it was something else. No warning, just get in the car and let's go, Will, this is your home now.

It wasn't fair! I couldn't even write Dad a letter, let him know I was all right—find out for sure if he was all right or if they'd lied to me about that. I wouldn't put it past them.

Then, suddenly, thinking of Dad, I got mad at him, too, and that hardly seemed fair. I remembered that night in the Santa Fe State Police building, Dad walking in, looking at me with that carefully blank expression. He probably had no idea why he'd been called to come in, didn't know if I'd been in a car wreck, or what. So he came in a little warily, not knowing what to expect, to see me sitting there on that bench with both hands raw and torn from Joe's face again and the blood that had poured out of my own nose still not washed off my face, only to have that damn nosy cop come wandering in with his printouts. Dad didn't say anything, I remember that. Just stood there with that same unreadable expression while two cops slapped a pair of handcuffs on him and led him away to "wait" somewhere else while they figured out exactly what was going on.

Dad didn't deserve my anger. What happened was because of Dave and Charlie.

And me.

He'd warned me, hadn't he?

"... You start something here, and the state cops will finish it for you..."

I should have left right then and there, man. Gotten out of that bar, away from the dance...

But, hey! It wasn't *my* fault. Who could have predicted that fight? Or a cop taking our prints to scare us and running them through a computer out of boredom? Nobody. The only reason the cops had my fingerprints in the first place was a first-grade field trip to the police station where they fingerprinted all the kids in the class. They were trying to get every kid's fingerprints on file just in case... Just in case they got kidnapped.

Like Dad did to me.

Which is why I kept getting mad at him when I thought about it. Dave and his long drive home kept hammering it in. Different car, different "father," same circumstances. It *hurt* when Dad came and got me. Maybe Dave hadn't been all that quick to find me, but he was the only father I had ever known, and I loved him.

Then, I mean.

I didn't know what I meant myself anymore.

An idea came to me then that I didn't care for much. I thought about what it was like, all that first year with Dad. The traveling life of the rodeo was different from anything I ever even imagined before. We'd be in Cheyenne one night and Reno the next, strange towns, strange people, a carnival atmosphere night after night. Once I knew I couldn't do much about getting back home, I let the excitement of those rodeo nights sweep over me. Fun, yeah, lots of fun. But scary and unsettling too. The only familiar thing in my life, almost, was Dad. If he had taken me straight to Monte Verde, straight to a new house and a new school maybe things would have been different, I wouldn't have been so completely dependent on him that I had to accept him as quickly as I did. I couldn't help but wonder if he realized how much I would come to need him, and therefore *have* to accept him in the turbulent traveling life he thrust me into, if that was another of his carefully laid plans, or if it just worked out that way—to his advantage.

A sudden tap-tap against the glass startled me so bad I jumped. I looked up warily, expecting one of those Claw guys from camp-out horror stories, at least. What I saw was a cop, bending down and tapping his nightstick against the window. Oh, marvelous.

I rolled down the window and said as politely as possible, "Yes, sir?"

"You all right, son? Having any problems?"

"No. I'm... uh... I had an argument with my dad," I said, which wasn't that far from the truth. "I just went for a drive to cool off."

"Uh-huh. You mind stepping out of your car, please. And, I'd like to see your license, registration, and proof of insurance."

He thought I was drunk, especially when he got a look at the spurs I was still wearing, but I passed all his tests easy enough. Finally he decided to let me go without a ticket or anything, since technically, there didn't seem to be any law against getting mad as long as all you did about it was sit alone in a dark place and think. He followed me, though, halfway back to the city before he turned around finally and went back to his own town. Once he was out of sight behind me, I flipped a finger at the rearview mirror. Just doing his job, I'm sure, but I was sick of cops just doing their jobs. Like Charlie Silva.

I'd memorized the turns I took to get out there, so it wasn't hard to find my way back to the city, and eventually back to Hawthorne. I noticed that I'd missed curfew by about fifteen minutes, but didn't think too much of it. I felt sort of relaxed, really. Flipping a finger at that cop had been so stupid I found myself laughing at it a moment later, and after that the anger that had been caroming around inside me without focus eased off some. I felt almost peaceful sliding along the quiet, dark streets that last bit of the way home.

The lights were all on when I drove into the driveway. I put the car into the garage, locked everything up city-tight, and let myself in the back door. Dave was standing there, waiting. I opened my mouth to apologize for being late, but I never got a chance.

"You're grounded, mister," Dave said flatly.

I thought about mentioning that I'd have been here earlier but for the cop, and decided that was maybe not the best excuse, with Dave glaring at me like the Wrath of God. In fact, his attitude pissed me off. It wasn't like I was all that late that he had to be standing here, waiting to punish me.

"For fifteen minutes?" I said instead.

"For lying to us about who you were with, for taking off who knows where from the dance... Cecilia said you left the gym at ten-thirty. That was more than two hours ago, almost two and a half. I was about ready to call the police, but I thought I'd give you the benefit of the doubt..."

"Some benefit!"

"That's enough! I really feel that I've been more than fair with you. I've even given you some breaks, let things slide that I should have been more strict about. I thought you needed time to adjust. Well, you've had time. I think what it is you need is more discipline. You've gotten into habits of just doing whatever strikes your fancy, and I can't tolerate that. Your actions affect too many other people, and I don't think you stop to think about those people before you choose your actions."

"I don't know what your gripe is," I said. "I didn't do anything tonight that deserves this! I didn't lie to you about who I was with, Cecilia made up her own story before I got a chance to say anything..."

"You didn't correct her though, did you? Why

couldn't you just say you were seeing Diana Rodriguez instead of Diana Cuthbertson?"

"What do you care? You don't know either of those girls! Cecilia thought I was taking out the daughter of a shrink and an M.D., and everybody was thrilled. Turns out I was with an orphan from the wrong side of the tracks, and I'm grounded?"

"That's not why..."

"Isn't it? If her name was Smith instead of Rodriguez would I still be grounded?"

"You're grounded for the lie, for breaking curfew, for taking off without telling anyone where you went, not for who you went out with."

"I didn't lie! And I'm only a few minutes late. I didn't mean to miss getting back here, but I went..."

"I don't want to hear your excuses. You're grounded, and that's that. And I want to remind you about doing things for the wrong reason. If you're seeing this Rodriguez girl just to get a rise out of me, she's the person who gets hurt. You understand that?"

I just stared at him, feeling my mouth drop open, but unable to think of anything to say. He thought I was taking Diana out to irritate him?

"I'm not 'seeing' Diana!" I said finally. "We're just friends! I have a girlfriend back in Monte Verde. Remember that place? The one where my life is? Incidentally, *her* name is Rodriguez, too!"

"I don't care," Dave said. "You take everything I say and twist it around like it's a personal attack. Maybe staying home all weekend you'll have a chance to think that over a little and realize that I'm just trying to help. Go on upstairs and get in bed now."

Trying to help? People who are trying to help, listen, they don't just talk. I opened my mouth to tell him that, then shut it. If he cared, he'd have listened the first time. If he cared, he'd have found me the first time. I went upstairs to my room without saying anything.

THIRTEEN

I closed my eyes when I heard the door open, figuring if she thought I was asleep, she'd go away. Didn't work, though. I felt more than heard soft steps coming across the carpet, then the bed dipped as she sat down on it. Mom. I knew that even before she reached out and brushed at my hair. Like she always does. I gave up and opened my eyes.

"Hi," she said.

"Hi," I said.

"Are you all right?"

"Marvelous," I said. "Can't you tell?"

"Your dad said you wouldn't talk to him when he came in to see you a little while ago."

"He doesn't want to hear anything I've got to say. Why should I bother?"

"Sweetheart. Listen. You understand, don't you, that when your father decides on a punishment, it's decided. That's all there is to it. I don't come by and change the rules he makes any more than he does that when I make rules. That's the way it's always been."

"I know."

"Okay. I'm not here to say I disagree with his decision or to sympathize with you. You were late."

Fifteen lousy minutes, I thought, but I didn't say anything.

"I just want to tell you something," she went on.

"Go ahead."

"It's just that... Well, when you watch a child grow from infancy to almost adulthood, the time goes so fast. It may seem like a lifetime to the child, but to the parent... you can't believe how fast it goes. It's hard to know, even after watching him grow, how to treat a sixteen-year-old: not an adult yet, but not a child anymore, either. It's trial and error with all parents. No one has all the answers, even if they have more than one kid, because kids are all different."

"So?"

"So. We have an even more difficult situation here, honey. We didn't watch you grow up. We knew you as a ten-year-old, and here you are all of a sudden, sixteen. What happened in the years you were gone? We don't know. What are you like now? We don't know that either, really. And, to further complicate things, we have another sixteen-year-old in the house already. When Cecilia comes in late, we have to punish her, right away. She does it on purpose, to see how much she can get away with. If we don't punish the five minutes she was late one night, the next night it'll be ten, or fifteen, then half an hour... next thing you know, she doesn't have any curfew at all, she's making up her own rules, and that's not right. You told your dad you haven't had curfews at all before, and the first night you went out, you came back late. With our experience with sixteen-year-olds, there's only one way to deal with that kind of behavior, do you understand?"

"No," I said.

"Come on, Billy," she said gently. It was a concession, using that name. She was giving a little, and she expected some give right back. I sat up.

"Couldn't he have grounded me tomorrow?" I asked. "Or next week?"

"Does it matter so much?"

"Yes, it does! I promised Rodrigo and his family I'd be out to help them today. Dave made me break that promise, he won't even let me use the phone to call up and explain why I'm not there. That's not right. That's not punishing me, that's punishing a whole bunch of people he doesn't even know! Dad would never have done anything like that to me!"

Her eyes were dark. It hurt her when I called my dad, "Dad." I didn't want to hurt her. But he was my dad.

"I'll talk to him," she said. "About letting you use the phone. But, what I'm trying to tell you is that we need time, okay? We need time to get used to you. You need time to get used to us again, too. Do you understand, honey?"

"Sure," I said, although really, I didn't. She smiled and patted my leg and stood up.

"You can come downstairs for lunch."

"I thought I had to stay in my room all day."

"You're not allowed to have food upstairs, and I won't permit anyone in this family to miss a meal for any reason. I already did talk to your dad about that. Half an hour, and you come down. It'll be ready."

Monday morning when I walked into homeroom, the teacher handed me a note that said I had an appointment with the guidance counselor for one o'clock. Probably wanted to check on me again, now that they had all my records, I thought. The note came with a hall pass, and at the proper time, I left the class I was in, and hiked down to the office corridor.

"Well, Mr. Campbell," Lawson said, when I came in. "How are things going for you at school? Any problems?"

Yates is a jerk, I thought. *Childress is after me because he doesn't like my boots. Conrad, the math teacher, is trying his best to flunk me.* "No. No problems."

"Getting along all right then?"

"Yeah. Fine."

"I imagine it's been quite an adjustment for you," he said. "Your records indicate the high school you left had a total of three hundred and forty-three students. That's quite a change from that to our school here."

"Yeah. A real change."

"You're not having trouble, though, finding your way around, or making new friends?"

"No."

"I understand that you're having a few problems at home, though."

"No," I said, but I was suddenly more alert. Who had he been talking to?

"It is true, isn't it, that you haven't seen the Campbells for over five years? It seems to me that that would cause a little friction in any circumstances."

"In any circumstances?" I asked. "Did Dave Campbell call you?"

"As a matter of fact, he did. Do you have a problem with that?"

"Yes!"

"Why?"

"Because it's none of your business."

"I'm here for any student who needs a little help adjusting..."

"I don't need help," I said.

"Your father called me and asked me..."

"David Campbell is not my father. My father is a man named Bill Melendez. Did you talk to any Bill Melendez?"

"No. I didn't. You seem a little upset about this to me. Why does it bother you so much?"

"I already told you. It's none of your business. They may hire you to talk to students, but there's no law that says I have to sit here and take this."

I got up and walked out, heading toward the student center. Only, I didn't go to the student center. I went out the front doors. I left. Dave thought I needed help, was that it? Called some jerk at the high school to talk to me about my problems? *Dave* was the problem.

I didn't go home. If I wanted to go home, I'd have just hung around the student center and waited for the bus. I wasn't skipping class to skip class, I skipped class because I needed to get away. Oh, man, I was mad! If I went back to class now, I'd kill somebody. Swear to God, I would.

I got as far away from the school as I could, walked over three miles just to be moving. I didn't plan on going anywhere. The only reason I even went into the little honky-tonk down by the tracks was because they had a pool table. There was a pool table in Sal's Bar and Cip and I played games there a lot. Like I told Dave, Sal's Bar was practically the Delgados' living room, so walking into a place that had neon beer signs against the walls and a bar across one end didn't feel like anything evil to me. It felt like going home. I didn't even order a beer, just a Coke, and went to play a game with some drunk who was back there playing alone.

Tinny country music, low lights, stale beer odors, and blinking neon were actually a little relaxing. It felt more natural than the enormous, bright-lit, brand-new school building I was running away from. I was considering what I was going to do about Dave calling the counselor on me when a cop walked in and busted me.

"You were trying to convince me not too long ago that you don't hang out in bars a lot," Dave said.

I didn't comment on that. I figured it didn't matter

what I had to say. Like Friday night, he'd already made up his mind.

"You don't have anything to say in your own defense?"

I just looked at him, keeping silent.

"I really don't understand this. I thought we started out so well, but time has made things worse, not better."

He sighed, and did a great imitation of a tired old man. Must be, having a kid like me around made people old before their time.

"I have to ground you," he said, like I was twisting his arm or something. "Two weeks for skipping school, two weeks for going down to the bar. A month."

"I can count," I said, speaking for the first time since I got home.

"Yes. I'm sure you can. Count on this, Will. This kind of behavior is not going to be tolerated. You may be used to keeping your own hours and going to school whenever it suits you, but that will not be permitted here. Go up to your room now and finish your homework."

"I don't have any."

"Go on, Will. Just go."

"I wish to hell," I said, "that I could."

Cecilia's locker was near our homeroom, since she got her assignment before school even started. Mine was way down some dark side corridor that led to the shop classes and the back side of the auditorium. When we got off the bus together Tuesday morning, Cecilia walked with me to my locker instead of saying good-bye, and splitting, like she usually did.

"It sort of bothers me the way you and Dad fight all the time," she said.

"Me, too."

"I'm really sorry about Friday night."

"It was nothing that you did."

"Yeah, but it was, really. See, I broke curfew, too. I got in . . . I don't know, not five minutes late, I'm sure. But Dad jumped on me right away. He always does. Once I was one minute late and I said my watch and his didn't keep time exactly the same. He said next time I should synchronize watches before I left the house! Anyway, I had big plans for Saturday, and I didn't want to get grounded and miss out, so when he started yelling at me, I just said, 'Yeah, what about Billy?' I knew you weren't back yet because the car wasn't there. And . . . well . . . I didn't think he'd land on you that hard."

"Déjá vu," I said.

"What?"

"Haven't we had this conversation before? In another life? You've always done that to me, Cecil! You get in trouble, and you point out something I'm doing, and then you get off the hook completely while I get blasted!"

"Yeah," she said, grinning. "Funny, ain't it? After all this time, it still works!"

"I should have guessed."

"You're not mad then?" she asked.

"Well, yeah, I'm mad! What do you think? I had plans for the weekend too, you know."

"I'm sorry."

"Yeah, yeah. Listen, could you just, maybe, like, stop it? Before I have to kill you or something."

"Sure. Maybe. But it was such a great scam!"

She waited while I unlocked my locker. In my old school, the lockers were normal locker width and half-high. I had a bottom locker half the time, which meant I was always crawling around on the ground to get my stuff. I hated it. Here, though, the lockers were full height, but only half as wide as normal. Then, to make sure you could fit all your big, fat textbooks in them, they had a pair of short book lockers on top of every pair of lockers, as wide as a pair of the skinny lockers and about ten inches tall. My book locker was the top one of the pair. The guy next to me, with the bottom book locker, was six feet three inches tall. Typical, right? I hung up my coat, then set my cowboy hat inside the book locker where I usually kept it. I got out the books I needed for morning classes and went with Cecilia to her locker.

"Do you skip classes a lot?" Cecilia asked as we cut through the student center toward homeroom. "I mean, did you, back in New Mexico?"

"No. Never."

"How come you did it yesterday? Dad was pissed. I've never seen him so mad!"

"I don't know what the big deal was. I only missed forty-five minutes of class. Writing, yet. I've never gotten lower than ninety-six in that class, it's not like those lousy forty-five minutes are going to break me or anything. If I was flunking, I could see it, but I'm not. So, what's his beef?"

I'd gone to the counselor's office during fifth hour, but it was over by the time I left. I always spent sixth hour in the student center catching up on homework, so I only missed last period when I walked out.

"Skipping is skipping. No matter what your grade is, it's against the rules, and you know how Dad is about rules. You'll probably get a couple weeks worth of detention study hall for that, too."

"So what? I can do homework in there as easy as I can in the other study hall."

"Uh-uh. They make you write lines."

"Lines?"

"Like, 'I will not skip seventh-hour classes again' umpteen million times."

"That's ridiculous! There's usually more bad students than great students in detention study hall; they ought to let them study."

"The voice of experience here! You get a lot of detention study hall before you moved here?"

"Couple times."

"For fighting?"

"No. You get suspended for fighting."

"Did you get suspended a lot?"

"Three times, Cecil. Three times in what? Four years? Once Joe Gallegos beat me up, once we scuffled a little in the parking lot, and three days before the dance I cracked him good."

"How did your other dad feel about that? You get suspended here, Dad'll murder you. He'll build stocks and set you out in the front yard for a week. He'd freak if you got suspended from school."

"Dad was pissed," I said. And he was that last fight just before the dance. But then I recalled the first time Joe and me got into a fight.

I was new in school, scared, lonely, lost. I had been standing in front of my locker trying to remember what the combination was, when Joe came by and smacked me on the back of the head so hard my nose banged into the locker door. That was it, man, the last straw. I dropped my books and spun around and punched him as hard as I could. He beat the crap out of me.

My first day of school, and they decided to expel me. Not suspend, expel. When the principal came to bust it up, Joe, who was killing me at the time, sat down and started screaming that I broke his arm. Fat chance. Dad called long distance from the hospital in Arizona where he was still in bed and in traction, to bawl out the principal and demand he let me back in school immediately. I was new, he told them, I was scared, I had never been to a high school before, and Joe started it anyway. Give a kid a break, huh?

Imagine Dave defending me like that, I thought.

"Yeah, but what'd he do?" Cecilia asked, referring to this last time, I was sure, not years back.

"What is this obsession you and Dave have about capital punishment? What did he *have* to do to me? I mean, I hit Joe, yeah, but I got suspended from school. I missed a test in history, dropped my grade average down from one hundred even to eighty..."

"Big deal!"

"Eighty's a B, it blew a perfect record! Besides which, I got a reputation with the principal, my girlfriend broke up with me and wouldn't speak to me for a week. Isn't that punishment enough?"

"Well . . ."

"I had to tell Dad what I did too, which was miserable. Dad always expected a lot from me. You screw up and you have to look at this huge disappointment, and you know what? That hurts! What do you want anyway, blood?"

"Dad would."

"He's got this idea that I've been raised by wolves or something since he last saw me, like I'm totally out of control because Dad didn't take a horsewhip to me every time I made a mistake. Dave raised me longer than Dad did. What's he think now, that getting kidnapped gives you brain damage? I didn't walk out of that class because I'm so evil, I left because I was too mad to go in there and sit down and behave. I'd have cussed out the teacher if I stayed, or hit somebody! Do you know what Dave did?"

"Besides grounding you?"

"Of course besides grounding me! He called Lawson to have him talk to me privately about how I'm not adjusting fast enough to my new home."

"Are you kidding?" Cecilia demanded. The way she wrinkled her nose when she said it showed me she had much the same opinion of Lawson that I did, even before she added, "Lawson's an idiot! Why did Dad want you to talk to him?"

"I don't know. Maybe because I'm too wild for normal parents to control."

"Oh, stop whining!" Cecilia snapped, as she popped her locker open. I held her books while she got out of her coat and hung it up. "Maybe I could talk to Dad," she added.

"Please don't! You've done enough."

"No. Really. I could explain things to him..."

"Mom says I should just give it time," I said. Cecilia took her books back, and looked at me.

"Billy," she said, seriously. "You don't even want to be here with us, do you?"

"I don't know. I miss my old home and my friends ...and Dad. Sometimes I miss Dana so much I can't even sleep nights. You're my family, too, though," I added, seeing her look at me with those deep blue eyes. "Or, you were once. I missed you guys."

"I missed you, too," she said. Then she grinned, and made it all a joke by adding, "With you gone, there was no one to tattle on to get myself out of trouble!"

FOURTEEN

Wednesday, I went to my locker after the final bell to get my stuff and found Diana waiting there for me.

"Hi," she said. "I didn't see you in study hall yesterday."

"I have detention study hall for the rest of the week," I said. Cecilia had been right, both about the punishment and what they expected you to do in there. Lines, for crying out loud!

"Yuck!" she said. "I had that once. Smarted off to the math teacher. My math teacher's such a joke though. I *am* flunking the class, but I really think it's his fault, not mine. Anyway, I heard you got grounded over the weekend, and I was kind of worried . . . I mean, it wasn't because of something I did, was it?"

"No. I took off with Dave's car after I dropped you, and I was late getting home."

"Rumors, rumors," she said. "I was wondering because when *I* heard the story, you and me both took off and vanished for two hours alone after the dance, which is really doing wonders for my reputation."

I was used to rumors. In a small town, everybody knew everything about you, but I was surprised at how fast and how twisted the story had spread in a school of this size. Maybe it was the size that twisted things.

"Great," I said.

"No big deal," she said with a shrug.

"It *is* a big deal! I'm so sick of people making assumptions. Or even making up stories from scratch! Why can't everyone just mind their own business!" I punched my locker door.

"Hey, take it easy. Really. Gossip's gossip, it never did mean anything." Then she looked at me again, cocking her head to peek up under the brim of my hat. "You're mad about something else, aren't you?"

"I got to go," I said.

"The buses aren't all here yet. I checked. What happened?"

I sighed and turned, leaning back against my locker. I didn't want to tell her. On the other hand, I did, mainly because after all the talking I did at the dance Friday, she knew better than anyone else around here what I was feeling.

"I got a letter..."

"From Dana?"

"From a friend of mine. Cipi Delgado. He said he felt obligated to tell me because we were such good friends... but it wasn't any of his business, you know? Dana should have told me herself—if there *is* anything to tell."

"More gossip," she said, nodding sympathetically. "Bad?"

"It was a Friday, at a dance, we made up again. The next Friday, so I hear, she went to another dance with another guy."

"I'm sorry," she said. She sounded like she really was, too.

"It's just this gossip! You hear these things, but can you believe it, you know? Dana hasn't written to me, that's true enough, but what would she be doing, going out with Joe Gallegos?"

"I don't know. Who's Joe Gallegos?"

"The slime bag of the whole school."

I was beginning to hate getting letters from home. The only one who wrote was Cip, and he was like some doomsayer, giving me only bad news. Like I didn't have enough problems here, I had to get letters like that from him.

"Hey, cowboy. Get off my locker!"

The skinny lockers were a whole lot narrower than I was. When I leaned back on my locker to talk to Diana, I was taking up more than just my own locker. I hadn't meant to bother anyone, but there wasn't anyone close by at the time. My six-foot-plus locker partner had just shown up, though. I started to straighten up and move away, but he didn't wait. He just shoved me sideways, which made me slam into the open door of the locker two down and hit the guy getting his stuff out of it with the door. He cussed me out.

"Oh, shut up," I said, irritated that he was cussing me when it was the other guy that did the shoving.

"Yeah, who's gonna make me?"

It wasn't worth an answer. I just turned my back on him. I was going to invite Diana to walk to the front doors together and get out of all this, when the guy I'd run into shoved me hard with both arms out straight. Wham! I was beginning to feel like a Ping-Pong ball, which did nothing much for the mood I was in. I was cussing already when I was slammed into the locker door of my giant-sized neighbor. His door slammed against him when I hit it, too. He came out from behind it, red-faced and angry.

"You son of a bitch stupid half-breed cowboy! Can't you even walk?"

"Billy!" Diana said sharply, like she thought I was going to get into a fight over that. I wouldn't. It wasn't worth it.

I started to draw in a breath, to let her know it was okay, but before I even did that, the Giant said, "You keep out of this, bitch!"

Why do guys always have to drag a girl into their arguments? He could have called me anything he wanted, I wouldn't have done a thing. But the sudden flash of surprise and pain in Diana's copper-colored eyes was more than I could take. I spun around and broke his nose.

Pissed?

Oh, man! Dave was out of control.

"Are you proud of yourself?" he yelled at me.

Proud? Of hurting someone like that? What a stupid question! That guy was big, but he'd never been smacked like that before. Noses *hurt.* I know that from personal experience. And they bleed like crazy, too. The blood covered the whole front of his shirt in the few seconds that everyone stood there in the hall staring in shock, even before someone hollered and the shop teachers all came running out to break it up.

They called the *cops.* Apparently, about the same time they built this lovely new school to take care of all the nice suburbanite kids, they also built a new police station right across the street. So, when they had trouble, they called the cops. It was convenient for them, but it didn't improve matters any that the cop who came to look into the fight was the same one who had busted me in the bar two days before. Dad had warned me about getting a reputation with the cops, and so had Charlie Silva. But then, I hadn't *planned* on getting in trouble. Who calls the cops for a simple fight at the school grounds? Not that that was any excuse. There was no excuse. Two dads had pounded that into me long, long ago.

"There are reasons and there are excuses," Dave Campbell had told me over and over when I was little. "You may have the best reasons in the world for something you did, but that doesn't excuse the behavior."

"You are responsible for anything you choose to do," Dad told me. "You might not like the choice you got, you may have good reasons for making your choice, but once you make it, it's yours. You can't lay it in anyone else's lap. Ever."

But, here was Dave, standing over me and yelling, "What sort of an excuse can you have for doing something like that?"

I didn't bother to answer, just sat there on the sofa, staring down at the hat I held in both hands.

He hadn't said much at the school, or on the way home. Maybe if he had, all the anger wouldn't have exploded out in saying stupid things once we were all in the living room. Cecilia was there, keeping her mouth shut, but biting her lips as she looked from Dave to me and back again. Mom sat near me, and every now and then a hand reached out toward me. Mom was a toucher. She always had been. Now though, it was like she couldn't decide what she wanted to do more, comfort me, or appease Dave. The hands always slipped back into her lap before they reached me.

"Of all the stupid, asinine, inexcusable . . . What am I supposed to do about this? You broke that kid's nose, do you realize that? Broken! Do you know what it means to break a nose?"

I didn't answer that either. Maybe he just never noticed my nose had that bump in the middle of it now that it didn't have before. I broke my nose crashing off a horse, not in a fight, but I still knew what it meant.

"I want to know what happened," Dave said. He was still mad, but he shifted suddenly onto a new track. I looked up, wondering what this new track was, but suddenly I realized he wanted details so he could find something in the other kid's behavior that might make it understandable, if not all right, that I hit him. No way I was getting into that! I went back to staring at my hat.

"William, I'm speaking to you. What happened?"

"Some of the kids said Brian Anderson was shoving him around and calling him names," Cecilia said.

"I'm not interested in what some of the kids said, I'm interested in what Will has to say. If anything."

Smug, that sounded. Either I was a criminal, or I would defend myself. What a choice!

"What happened?"

"I hit him because I'm a juvenile delinquent," I said.

"Is that supposed to be a joke?"

"I'm not laughing. I'm just telling you what you want to hear. You can't control me because I spent too much time away, and Bill Melendez wasn't as good a father as you were. My daddy just raised me too rough." Charlie Silva's words, almost rote, came out, and I remembered as I said them what I had answered Charlie: *"You can't blame my dad. I've only known him five years."*

"You think that's what I want to hear?"

"Isn't it?"

"What I want to hear is the truth, Will..."

"Billy! And you don't care about the truth. I've tried to tell you things before, but you just shake your head at how awful it is to have a criminal like me in the family and you hand out your punishments without ever listening!"

"I'm listening now."

"You're not listening! You're waiting for me to say something I can hang myself with; that's not the same!"

"I take it you think I've been unfair with you lately?"

"From the start!"

"You don't think that perhaps you feel that way because you're used to doing things without any discipline and you find the new rules restricting?"

"No. I didn't run away from home, you know. You may resent the fact that I spent the last few years with my natural father, but I did spend them with him. I wasn't hopping freights with the other hobos or begging handouts in Times Square."

"Tell me then," Dave said. "Just what would this... Melendez... have done in a situation like yesterday? How did he handle things like skipping classes and wandering around honky-tonks, gambling with drunks?"

Gambling! I started to protest that, and decided, since he had asked about Dad, I wouldn't change the subject and let him off the hook.

"You want to know what he'd do? He'd do nothing!"

"That's exactly what I've been talking..."

"Yeah, just what I thought. Jumping to conclusions. You don't even want to know why!"

"*Why* isn't important, Will..."

"*Billy!* He wouldn't have done anything because that would never have happened! Why do you assume the worst? What is it about me that you look at me, and you see some sort of criminal? Dad never treated me like that! He knew I didn't break rules just to break them! I never skipped a class before not because I thought it was that big a deal honestly, but because you don't get college scholarships by being an off-and-on student. Dad knew that. He also knew that if he had something to say to me, he could say it. He never sent me to some counselor, like you'd send a car out to a mechanic to fix when it didn't run the right way to suit you."

"I didn't send you away to be fixed," Dave said. "I

thought since you weren't interested in talking to me, it might be easier..."

"Not interested? Damn! Not interested! I talked to you for hours on the road. Answered all your questions. When we got here, though, all you were interested in was discipline. It didn't matter what I had to say, you had to pass out the discipline. That was more important."

"It may seem that way to you sometimes, but that's only because I care very much about you, and about what happens to you."

"BULLSHIT!" I yelled at him.

"It's hard for you to understand..."

"It's not hard for me to understand anything! I'm not stupid, you know. Dad's name was printed right there on my birth certificate. It's not like we were living in a foreign country under an assumed name or anything."

"Are you saying that five years ago we didn't try hard enough to find you?"

"You didn't try at all! You were probably glad to be rid of me. No more embarrassing family mistakes hanging around the house! You didn't show up until the cops called you and told you you had to."

"That's not true," Dave said. "That's not true at all. We do love you, very much. And we tried hard to find you..."

"Real hard, yeah. You couldn't wait to move so I couldn't find you if I ever did get back. Man, if you cared half as much as you're trying to convince me you do, you'd have adopted me legal!"

FIFTEEN

Mom was crying. Cecilia, for once in her life, kept her mouth shut. Dave turned and walked out of the room, and I knew with a sudden stab like a stake pounding through my heart that it was true. Some part of me had always hung on to the idea that Dad had lied about that. Some part of me had never stopped loving Dave and Becky Campbell, and wanting them to love me, too. A small part. Dead now.

I picked up the hat I hadn't realized I'd dropped and sat with my elbows on my knees, staring down at it.

Dave came back. He had an envelope in his hand, and he opened it up and pulled out a thin sheaf of documents.

"Take it," he said, shoving it under my nose. I did. "Read it."

I glanced at it. Saw my name. Started reading. Legal adoption papers. William James Trevor, hereafter known as William James Campbell, with a whole lot of rigmarole in between, stamps and seals and notary marks. Dated . . . two weeks after the day I was born.

"We never pretended that you were our natural child," Dave said. "That would have been stupid. Anyone who can count knows that can't be right. You and Cecilia are only five months apart. But I can't imagine why you seem to have this feeling that you're not a regular part of this family. You are and you always have been. That's why it cuts me so bad to hear you call Melendez 'Dad.' Technically you could argue that he caused your birth, but I'm the one who raised you and loved you and took care of you from the day you were born. Even if it took a few days for the paperwork to go through to make you legal, you have always been *my* son. Do you understand that? You can call yourself Will or Billy or Fred Flintstone, you are still my son."

"I thought . . ." I said, and hesitated, staring at the papers.

"You thought what?"

"That you just . . . that you were, like, watching me. For Aunt Margaret. For a favor."

"She did ask us to, actually. Not because she didn't want you, Will, but because she wanted what was best for you. But we all agreed, Margaret, your mother and I, that what was best for you was *not* being part of two families, and belonging to neither of them, but belonging to one family: ours. That's why we adopted you, that and the fact that we wanted you very much. See, this way, Margaret could still see you, but as an aunt, same as she is to Cecilia, and you would have a whole family. The four of us, we're a family, Will, and you've always been a part of that. Always."

"He told me . . . Dad said if you'd really wanted me back, you could have found me easy. You could have, too. I know."

"We did try," Dave said. "Please believe that we did. We didn't just wait for the police either, we hired a private detective. He told us one of the ways to trace missing children is by school records. Find a kid the right age, newly registered in the right grade. But you skipped a grade. That's why we were a little upset when you told us about that. It's not that we weren't proud of you, we were. Are. But it was a bit of a shock."

I shrugged. It seemed to be just an evasion to me, anyway. "Yeah, sure. If you had nothing else to go on."

"We didn't actually have much, just a description of the man who had taken you," Dave said.

"And his name."

"We didn't know at that time . . ."

"Oh, come on! You told me yourself you knew who my dad was before I was even born! You not only didn't look, you left town to make sure I couldn't get back. I called. The number was disconnected. I wrote. No such person at this address. Just like Dad said!"

"Oh, my God!" Mom said. "I knew if we moved..."

"When was this?" Dave interrupted. "How long after you were taken?"

"Fourteen, maybe fifteen months," I admitted.

"Why did you wait so long?"

"I couldn't...It was the best I could do, okay? Anyway, what difference does it make? If I had a kid missing, and I had to move, I'd make sure there was a way that kid could get in touch with me. If I wanted him to."

"The police were still looking. They knew where to find us. And we took the precaution of telling the people who bought the house what had happened, so they could watch for you or for a letter from you after the post office stopped forwarding things. Someone just screwed up somewhere. I want to tell you I'm sorry, but I also want to yell at you for being so foolish. You should have gone to the police, you should have spoken to Charlie Silva. They'd have helped you. There's so many things you could have done."

"I did what I could," I said.

"And you still think we didn't?"

"It was right there all the time," I reminded him again. "In black and white."

"In hindsight," Dave said, "I can see we made a mistake about that. But at the time, we had a description of the man who had taken you, we were going mostly on that. Besides, I still can't figure out how he could possibly have known you even existed. Your Aunt Margaret had no contact with him at all after... Well, she knew him very briefly. How did he find out about you, do you know?"

"He said I was born in a hospital in Chicago," I said.

"Yes. Margaret was going to school there, the same university where she teaches now."

"Dad did a show in Chicago. He broke his leg and they took him to that same hospital. When he went to check out, the computer had eaten his records, so they put a search in the memory, for anything at all on Guillermo S. Melendez of Monte Verde, New Mexico. Instead of his bill, the computer spit out my birth record."

"Good God," Dave murmured, rubbing his eyes like they hurt. "And then he told you we didn't want you? That you weren't even adopted?"

I loved Dad. He'd taken good care of me. He always stood up for me. But I remembered again the first few weeks, the fear and the hurt...

"Yeah."

"You understand he had to, don't you? I don't know what he had in mind when he picked you up out of that ballpark, but I know what he got. A very stubborn, willful, independent young man. The only way he was going to keep you from running off and getting him hung was to keep you tied up all the time. He couldn't do it with chains. That would make the whole kidnapping pointless, wouldn't it? He tied you up with words, words a frightened ten-year-old might not believe, but that he'd remember, that would soak in, that would stay with him . . . I can understand that."

I couldn't. Dad had told me lies. Dave had used threats. Either way, I was sick of it, sick of people trying to program me.

I didn't say that though.

Dave sighed. He turned and walked over to the window and stood staring at it, though the drapes were pulled. Mom reached over to hold my hand, but I shook her off. I didn't mean to hurt her feelings, but I felt so mixed up inside, I didn't want her comfort. Comforting me now was like pulling me to their side of things. I felt pulled in half already.

"I'm going to go for a drive," Dave said suddenly. "You want to come with me, Will?"

"Uh. Yeah."

"But what . . . ?" Mom started.

"I don't know," Dave said. He picked up the overcoat he'd tossed on the armchair when he came in, and opened the door. I put on my hat and followed him.

We took the Ghia. West of town, Dave turned through a gate that led into a wooded area where there was a small lake with a road winding around it, in and out of autumn trees and dappled sunshine. Dave didn't say anything for a long time, and neither did I. I was too busy feeling things to worry about words. I realized quick enough that Dave was thinking things through, too. Back home when I needed to sort out my thoughts, I usually saddled up San Pablo and headed up into the mountains. The emptiness there made thinking somehow easier. There's nothing like open country to calm the spirit, to let the boiling slow down so that you can think, even if the things you have to think about are things you don't want to know.

SIXTEEN

"About the time you disappeared," Dave said slowly, picking his words carefully, "we were beginning to worry about how we were going to talk to you and Cecilia about sex. I went to the library and checked out some child psychology book to see what it had to suggest. The main thing I've always remembered from that book was where it said you should ask the child to describe the process to you first, so that you understand what sorts of ideas and misconceptions he might have already. Otherwise, you pile correct information on top of strange misinformation, and the end result might have very little to do with reality. We haven't been talking about sex lately, but I think if we'd followed the advice in that book, we wouldn't be where we are at the moment, either."

"You mean, like I have the wrong base ideas about things, so you can't load me down with new information?"

"No. I mean more like we both started out with some preconceived notions, some of them close to accurate, some of them wildly incorrect, and we've been trying to build from that when we should have torn the whole structure down and started from scratch. I should have kept you out on the road longer."

"No," I said. The word came out without me thinking, sharp and automatic. Dave smiled.

"The experience wasn't pleasant for you. I could see that and I wanted more than anything *not* to cause you any more pain. So I let you do things your way, jumping in with both feet instead of getting used to the water...isn't that how we described it at the time?"

"I don't know."

"Yes, you do. Don't be so contrary. The point is,

tearing down these misconceptions can be painful. Sparing the pain, I reinforced the problem. You're the one who brought up the subject of when we moved, back when we were still on the road. You were curious, I know now, because of that letter. You might have told me about it then, but you needed more time, and I rushed you."

"It's not that big of a deal. It was just a damn letter."

"It is a big deal, though. You know that. You spent the last five years believing that we didn't love you, that we didn't even want you, and because of that you built yourself a new life somewhere else. Now you're here again." He sighed and chewed on his lip for a moment, thinking, and I stared out the car window at the lake.

"Looking at an adoption paper isn't going to suddenly reverse five years of belief," Dave said finally. "Even if we had talked on the road, you'd still be struggling now, trying to assimilate this new information with five years of deeply imbedded feelings. I don't expect any instantaneous changes. But at least now I know what I'm fighting and where all the anger is coming from. All I can say is... I'm sorry. I just didn't know."

"You didn't ask," I said. "About anything. You never asked."

"I did at first. But it was too soon, I understand that

now. Will...Billy!" He shook his head. "It's going to be hard to get used to that."

"You don't have to," I said.

"Why not?"

Why not? Why did he have to ask? Now I had to think of the reason.

"He called me that," I said finally.

"Is that good or bad?" Dave asked.

"It's not good or bad. It's just that you're not m— You guys are two different people." I knew what I was feeling, I just didn't know how to explain it.

But Dave nodded. "That makes sense," he said.

"It does?"

"Yeah. It does."

We both went back to staring out the windows in silence for a while.

"How do you feel?" Dave asked.

"Confused, I guess, more than anything."

"We have to talk," Dave said. "You and I. We have to talk as much as we can. Basically, neither of us has really changed in the past five years, we're the same people, but we're both so much more than we were. Five years of experiences, five years of learning, that's a lot of growth. To deal with each other, we have to understand at least part of that growth."

"Yeah."

"I'm sorry about the counselor. I really thought it would help. I could feel your anger at me, and we weren't talking to each other. I thought maybe you'd find it easier to talk to some third party, someone not personally involved. There's no shame, you know, in getting counseling help. Everyone needs help with things now and then."

"Not Lawson," I said. "I can't talk about personal stuff with Lawson. Not ever."

"Okay. Can you talk to me?"

"Now?"

"Whenever you need to."

I thought about it, let another couple miles slip past.

"Did you talk to...your other father?" he asked finally when I didn't answer.

"About some things," I said. I'd talked to Charlie about love, I recalled. And I had never talked to anyone about how it felt to be jerked away from the life and family I'd always known and dumped in a strange place with strange people, not even to Dad. I looked up and saw Dave studying me out of the corner of his eye and I wondered if I'd ever tell him, either. Maybe. Some day. Maybe not. I was still so mad at him.

"I've been doing a little thinking about this punishment business," Dave said. "To go by the book, do you understand the purpose of punishment?"

"To teach right from wrong," I said. Rote answer,

memorized and forgotten years ago, uninteresting now.

"Right and wrong being what, exactly?"

That gave me pause. I thought it over and said, "When people live together in a society, there have to be certain . . . standards . . . of, uh . . . acceptable behavior . . . in order for them to get along with each other. Right and wrong, then, would be behavior that society in general considers acceptable or unacceptable."

"Okay," Dave said. "That's close enough." He was quiet awhile, organizing his thoughts. Finally he asked, "What's your opinion on this fight you got into?"

"My opinion?"

"Who's to blame, for one?"

"Me, obviously. I hit the kid."

"What should you do about that?"

"I don't know. I'd take it back if I could, but I can't. I could apologize, I suppose. Offer to pay to have his nose fixed."

"The insurance covered it, but you should apologize as soon as they let you back in school. Now, I want you to do something else. Pretend for a minute it was Cecilia who punched that guy. Imagine the same circumstances—which I still don't understand all that well, honestly."

"Cecilia wouldn't have hit him."

"Let's just say she did. What would she do when she got in trouble for it? Do you know?"

"No."

"I do. I've never had this particular situation come up before, but I have been dealing with this girl for sixteen years. I know exactly what she'd do. She'd stamp and whine and complain that it wasn't her fault. He pushed her or he called her names or he started it somehow, and it just wasn't her fault that he ended up with a broken nose. She *had* to hit him."

"That's ridiculous," I said, but I thought: *It sounds like Cecilia.*

"You were right about punishment being to help teach the difference between right and wrong. For little kids, that's true. For a kid your age, it's more to show you that whatever you choose, right or wrong, you're still responsible for it. Not Anderson. Not even me, mad as you may be at me, but you."

"I know."

"I know you know. I want to tell you now, you were right before. I have been unfair with you, because I've been treating you the way I treat Cecilia."

"Mom said something like that Saturday," I recalled.

"Good. Then you understand, don't you? She has to be punished, she has to learn these lessons. But you already know. So what am I supposed to do with you?"

"I don't know."

"You're not grounded," he said, after a minute.

"No?"

"I'm still upset about this business with skipping class and hanging out in a bar, but I understand how it came about, and I am partly responsible. You're not grounded for that anymore."

"What about for the fight?"

"I'm not ready to deal with that yet. I'll let you know in the morning. Meantime, I'd like to comment on last Friday night, while we're on the subject."

"Friday?"

"The dance."

"Oh. Yeah."

"I know you've been through some things these past few years that I can never fully comprehend. But look at this from my point of view for a minute, all right? I set time limits not because I don't trust you or I think that you need to learn responsibility, but because I like to know where you are and what time to expect you back so if something does happen I can start looking for you as soon as possible. Does that make sense?"

"Wilderness trips, that's a survival requirement, that someone knows where you went and how long you plan to be gone so if something goes wrong, they can find you."

"So, you understand what I mean?"

"Yeah."

"And can you also understand that I lost you once

already? That other time, I went from wondering why you were running late, to worrying, to calling the cops, to terror and a sense of loss I can't even begin to describe. When you broke curfew the other night, even though you were only a few minutes late, all those feelings came back in a rush, and I was so scared. I know it's wrong, and it's crazy, but it's also very common for parents who are worried sick about their child to have that worry explode in anger when the child turns up again, safe and sound."

"I've seen it happen," I said. "A relief reaction or something, right?"

"Right. That's what happened Friday. I went crazy, and you suffered for it all weekend. I'm sorry it happened. The best way we can avoid it in the future is don't break curfew. Save us both a lot of pain. Or, call and let me know you're safe and just running late. I'd accept that."

"Call," I said. "I keep forgetting how available pay phones are in the city."

Dave smiled. "We just have to remember to talk," he said. "I know this is a novel concept, but you really can tell me anything. If I don't understand..."

"Yeah?"

"I'll ask questions."

I found myself smiling, even though I was mad at him. I had been mad at him for a long, long time, I thought. Mad at him for not finding me when I needed him to, for not being there when I did try to get back. He had deserted me. At least that's how it felt for years. And then he came back and ripped away the comfortable new life I had, took it away without even an apology. I wasn't just mad at him, I hated him.

But sitting there next to him, with the setting sun throwing sparks off the surface of the lake, it was too easy to remember other things. Like Dave patiently pitching to me in the back yard every day after work till I finally started hitting the baseball. Like the way he came upstairs to check on us, Cecil and me, every single night. Mom always tucked us in, but Dad... Dave...came up before he went to bed to check and make sure we were all right. Always. Like walking down to the Mississippi River on a Saturday morning to go fishing. I never cared all that much for fishing, but I used to love it when he took me. It was just the two of us, Mom and Cecilia weren't invited. We'd lean up against the concrete rail, watch the bobbers way down below in the water, and talk.

In a way, it was easy to hate him for all the bad things that happened. But when I wasn't hating him, I remembered how much I loved him. Just like sometimes thinking how Dad hurt me, I forgot that I loved him. For a minute.

"Anything wrong?" Dave asked.

"I was just wondering..."

"Yes?"

"Do your relationships with other people ever get easier to understand? When you get older?"

"No," he said. "No, I think I can honestly say they never do."

"Gee. That's something to look forward to."

Dave laughed. Like Dad usually laughed at my sarcasms.

Dad and Dave. Bill and Dad. Two dads. I wondered who to be mad at now.

SEVENTEEN

Dave took the morning off work to go back to the school and have a conference with the principal. He took me along, though I had to sit outside in the car and wait. It took almost two hours.

"They're not going to expel you," he said when he came back. "They wanted to, but I talked them out of it."

Imagine Dave defending me like that, I'd thought, just two days ago. Live and learn.

"For one punch they were going to expel me?"

"You did break that boy's nose."

"Lucky shot."

"Maybe. Anyway, you walked out of classes Monday, and on Wednesday you broke someone's nose. It gave them all the impression you're not their kind of kid, if you see what I mean."

"Yeah."

"Anyway, this I know is going to make you mad, but I sort of snowed them about how much emotional pressure you're under right now due to this kidnapping and all..."

"Oh, man!"

"I didn't do it to embarrass you, Will. I did it because it was the only argument I thought was strong enough to move them, and I didn't want to see you expelled from school. Think of it as a good excuse. Just about the only excuse they'd accept, not to mention the fact that it happens to be true. Anyway, all you have is three days' suspension. But, you have to take F's on all your work for those three days."

"No tests, and most of my classes have weekly assignments, not daily. It shouldn't be too devastating."

"Your junior year is the one that colleges look at most closely when you go to apply, because you apply before the senior year is over. Don't screw up your junior year."

"I won't. I'll try not to any worse, anyway. Uh..."

"What?"

"I'm sorry about all the work you've had to miss the past couple days. I hope this won't get you into trouble, too."

"I'm glad that occurred to you, but I'm my own boss now. Don't you have any idea what I do for a living?"

"Uh. No. I guess not. Same thing you did five years ago?"

"Basically."

I thought about the little house, the old neighborhood, the million-year-old Impala Mom used to drive, and then this big fancy new house, the Ghia, the eight-foot-fence around the back yard for a pool. "Whatever you do, you must be getting better at it."

Dave laughed. "Why don't you come to work with me today? You didn't have any other pressing plans, did you?"

Dave was an independent managerial consultant. He had an office downtown somewhere, but that week he was spending most of his time out at a steel company where poor business management had nearly bankrupted the place. He was involved in reorganizing the staff and relocating office space and a lot of other stuff, shaking the company down from top to bottom to get rid of waste and excess spending. One of the old company bosses patted me on the back and said that they'd have gone under if it weren't for Dave. I watched him studying employee charts, and cost-to-production ratios, and plans for building steel water towers, and realized that he was very good at what he did. Whatever it was. It felt strange, watching him help professionals to run their own business. It was hard to say what the strange feeling was, at first, then I realized I was proud of him. It was the same feeling I felt for Dad sometimes. Strange enough having two dads. Stranger being proud of them both.

Wednesday when I went back to school I was late for first hour because the principal spent half an hour telling me why fighting wasn't permitted in school. I wondered if he seriously thought I believed that fighting *should* be allowed at school.

Yates pulled a pop quiz and seemed mad when I got 96 percent on it after missing three days. I discovered I was supposed to give an oral report in Spanish about Christmas customs in Spanish-speaking countries. The teacher said I could do it late and take a reduction of one grade, but I decided to wing it. I told about *Las Posadas, luminarias,* and *farolitos,* the fiesta of the Virgin of Guadalupe, and traditional treats of *biscochitos* and hot chocolate in early New Mexico, and got an A minus. The report, the teacher told me, was A quality, but it wasn't fair to the kids who put a whole week of work into theirs to give me an A for something I'd put so little into. I felt like telling her I'd put five years of my life into it, but I took the minus and shut up. It still counted as an A, after all.

In PE Thursday, basketball ended and we signed up for new activities. We had a choice of volleyball, basketball (again), gymnastics, and health, and since health was a requirement, I picked that to get it over with. It was a little unsettling, though, to walk into the classroom after lunch and have Coach Langley assign me a seat for the next six weeks right next to Brian Anderson. I had managed to avoid Anderson near the lockers all day, and was considering keeping that up for the rest of the year, but I couldn't avoid showing up for health class.

When I sat down, he scowled at me. On a guy that big, with tape all over his nose, a scowl was almost deadly. When class ended, I hurried to head him off just outside the door.

"Anderson!"

"What do you want?" he said.

"I want to apologize," I said.

"What?" He looked suspicious, like he thought I was putting him on or something.

"I...uh...I just broke up with my girlfriend, and I was a little on edge. You shouldn't have talked to that girl like that, but I shouldn't have hit you, either. I'm sorry. It won't happen again."

He didn't answer, just made a sound like a grunt and looked me carefully up and down—mostly down. Geez, that guy was huge!

"Why do you go around dressed like some cowboy all the time, anyway?" he said.

"I *am* a cowboy," I said.

"Oh." He looked down at me again. "Broke up with your girl, huh?"

"Yeah."

"Me, too," he said. He turned and hurried off to make it to his next class in the three minutes of passing period that were left. I did some hurrying of my own and slipped in just under the bell, feeling like a weight had been lifted. I didn't want to end up with a lifetime feud at this school like I had in Monte Verde. Joe Gallegos had picked on me every available chance after our first fight, and I guess I never did forgive him for the way he treated me when what I needed so desperately was more like a kind word or a friend. I was afraid I'd made another lifelong enemy in Anderson, and I was relieved to find I hadn't. I was already looking forward to talking to him again.

Saturday another package arrived for me from Monte Verde, a big brown cardboard box all taped up and with no return address.

"What's this?" Dave asked, when he saw it sitting in the kitchen.

"It's for Billy, but he won't open it," Cecilia said.

"Why not?"

I didn't want to. I didn't want to start anything again. Last time boxes came for me, Dave and I ended up shouting at each other. I knew he still wasn't comfortable with the saddle, or the gun that was carefully wrapped and stashed in the attic. There just wasn't anything else for anyone to send me, and the lack of a return address worried me too. What if it was from Dad? What if his sending it broke whatever agreements Charlie Silva and Dave had worked out? If it was from him, and I opened it, he could still go to jail.

That box scared me.

But, "Let's open it and see what it is, Will," Dave said. So, I carefully slit open all the packaging tape and everyone gathered around while I opened the box. Inside, there was a plastic bag that had a label: "CAUTION — DRY ICE!"

Mom used a pot holder to lift the bag out carefully,

though it looked like most of it had melted. Underneath was a letter.

Coyote,

I know you were angry when I saw you last. I can't blame you for that. But your Daddy was wrong when he took you from your family. You know that. You belong with them. You should have said something a long time back. I think of my little granddaughter, who always called me 'Daddy,' but had another one somewhere else. If he ever came to try and take her away from me, I'd kill him. Think of that when you think of this Dave Campbell. And remember. He was your Daddy before, wasn't he? He seemed like a nice man when I met him. A lot like your other Dad, the one you have here. You'll hurt for a while, I know, but think of it this way: you did get a chance to know both of them. You got a chance to live in two worlds, something not many people have.

Which is why I am sending you this package. Once you get used to New Mexico cooking, nothing else is quite the same, and I remember how hard it is to get authentic New Mexico food anywhere but here. So. Enjoy.

Remember us all here when you eat this, remember that we all cared for you, too, and we will think of you always.

Sincerely,
Carlos Luciano Silva y Velasquez

"What is this?" Cecilia asked. While I was reading the letter, she had started unpacking the box. "It's a package of dried cornhusks. Who would send a package of cornhusks through the mail?"

"It's for cooking," I told her. I set down the letter and looked into the box myself There were the cornhusks and a five-pound sack of *masa harina,* "dough flour" for making homemade tamales, a string of dried red chiles, two packages of red chile powder, a box of fresh green chile, four dozen blue corn tortillas, a sack of pinto beans, a packet of *chicos* to go in the beans, a sack of dried *posole,* and a whole pound of roasted piñon nuts. It was a care package. I just looked at it all and laughed.

"When you get all this stuff put away, grab your coat, Will," Dave said. "You have a job interview."

"I do?"

"Yes. I assume you're still interested in working after school. You did ask me once, but I said no without really thinking about it."

"Yeah. So, how come you changed your mind?"

"I suddenly remembered the other day why it was we put you in Little League when you were small. Not for the love of baseball—as I recall you were never that fond of it, but just because all the games and practice sessions kept you out of trouble. You've always needed more activity than most kids. Since you're not interested in school sports, I thought a job was a good idea, after all."

"What kind of job?"

"One that'll make you sweat a little, let you release some of the pressures you're under with good old-fashioned physical labor."

"But what...?"

"You'll find out when we get there."

Dave drove us to a place called Robins' Egg Stables, west of town. Up a steep, curving driveway, there was a small house, a large red barn, and a long, low stable, with several corrals out front. Dave parked next to one of the corrals and we both climbed out. A girl about twelve years old was bouncing around the corral on horseback, wearing jodhpurs, boots, a hunting jacket, and a helmet. A woman, dressed almost the same but hatless, was leaning on the railing yelling things at her. When we got out, she turned and came to meet us.

"Mr. Campbell," she said, shaking Dave's hand. She was a little taller than me, a lean, stringy woman of about forty, with a handsome face, a ramrod-straight back, and a cigarette hanging like a permanent fixture from the corner of her mouth.

"This is your son?"

"This is Billy, yes," Dave said, though he still called me Will at home. "Billy, Mrs. Lundquist."

"Pleased to meet you, ma'am," I said, doffing my hat. She held out a hand though, so I shook it, like Dave had. Instead of letting my hand go after shaking it, she turned it over and studied my palms.

"Used to hard work, are you?" she asked, dropping it finally, and I realized she'd been checking to see how soft the undersides of my hands were. Even after four weeks in the city, they weren't that soft. Years of hammers, axes, rakes, shovels, hoes, and saws had left their marks in hard ridges of yellow callus on both hands.

"Yes, ma'am."

"You always that polite?"

"Yes, ma'am."

She inhaled on her cigarette and blew smoke at me. "You know horses?"

"I don't know anything about this English riding stuff, but I've worked with stock before. I've wrangled horses on wilderness pack trips, and I spent some time with the rodeo."

"Mr. Campbell here, as I'm sure you know, tells

people how to run their own businesses. He tells me I need help, even though I keep telling him I can't afford it. Now, you convince me, Billy. Why should I hire you when there's a dozen little girls around here every day offering to sweep out and clean up for free just to be around horses?"

Good question. I looked around and considered a minute, then looked back at her. "Because I can do things those little girls can't."

"Oh? Like what?"

I bent to pick up a nail that had fallen out of the fence. "Carpentry work, for one. I've driven a back-hoe before too, so I bet I can run that tractor you have over there. And I can haul around hundred-pound bales of hay all afternoon if it's needed."

"I can only afford minimum wage, and maybe ten or fifteen hours a week."

"I get a lot more than minimum wage for things I'm good at, but I've never worked in a stable before, so minimum sounds fair."

"You'd be amazed what he can get done in fifteen hours a week, too," Dave said.

"Transportation?" the lady said.

"He goes to the high school on this end of town. I checked already, and one of their buses comes out this way. He can come on the bus after school, and either his mother or I can pick him up after work. If you need him weekends, I can make arrangements for that too."

"Every night after school, say from three-thirty to five-thirty or six, and half a day Saturdays," Mrs. Lundquist said.

"Sounds good to me," I said.

"You're here to do labor, not help with the lessons. You have no business being on any of the horses, or talking to any of my students. Is that clear?"

"Yes, ma'am."

"See you Monday, then."

"I'm hired?"

"Of course. Monday. Good afternoon, Mr. Campbell."

It wasn't the wilderness, but it was outdoors. The air smelled of horses and hay, rain and autumn leaves, and I already knew from personal experience Dave was right about physical labor being good for sweating out tensions. As Mrs. Lundquist walked off to yell at the little girl again, I turned and grinned at Dave.

"Thanks."

"Hey," he said shrugging. "Putting together management and labor teams that'll work is part of my job."

EIGHTEEN

The crowds I had expected for my homecoming arrived on Thanksgiving Day. The doorbell kept ringing and ringing, the house kept getting more full, more noisy, and I sat upstairs in my bedroom with my economics homework spread out on my desk.

Cecilia banged on the door and walked in without waiting to be asked. She said "Ugh!" as she walked in, same as always. The spaceships were gone, but Cecilia claimed the Mexican blankets I replaced them with made my room look like the lobby of a cheap dude ranch.

"When are you coming down?" she asked, flopping on my bed. "A lot of people want to know."

"I have to finish this."

"Do it tomorrow."

"I have to go to work tomorrow."

"Then do it... No, forget it. Anything I say you'll have an answer to. What are you really doing up here?"

I had to smile. "Thinking," I said.

Dad and I always had Thanksgiving dinner at Furr's Cafeteria in Santa Fe. I hated those dinners. Dad did, too. But neither of us could cook a turkey. Lack of family on family holidays always made me daydream about the Campbells. It made Dad think back, too, I know. I caught him once flipping through his old family photo albums afterwards when he thought I was asleep.

"Billy?"

"I was just thinking about Dad," I said.

"He's the one who sent me up here. He wants to know when you're coming down."

"My New Mexico Dad," I explained.

"You're becoming schizophrenic," Cecilia said.

I had started to get into the habit of calling Dave Campbell "Dad" again, but it got confusing sometimes. If I was thinking of New Mexico or the rodeo and Bill Melendez, I thought "Dad," automatically. If I thought about the Campbells, my new life, or Davenport and thought of Dave Campbell, the word "Dad" came to mind also. That's one of the things I liked about Diana. I spent last Saturday afternoon with her at her cousin's wedding dance, and we talked for hours. When I called two different people "Dad" at different times, she not only understood why, but always knew who I was talking about.

We'd had a good time at the dance, too. It still astounded me how pretty she could look when she took off her baggy overalls and traded them in for real girl clothes. She'd worn something long, lavender, and fluffy to the wedding. It made her look like one of those little china statues of angels they sell in card shops. She was a good dancer, too. She'd never danced *rancheras* before, or a country swing, but I led her through both, and she caught on quick.

"I thought maybe you were up here mooning about that girl of yours in New Mexico," Cecilia said.

"She's on my mind still, sure," I said. I had wanted to marry Dana, I recalled. But that seemed now like such a long time ago. "I guess the thing that still bugs me most is if she was going to dump me, why didn't she pick some decent guy? Why a bum like Joe Gallegos?"

"My guess is that in a little school like that, most of the decent guys were your friends, and they would want to know how you felt before picking up on your ex-girlfriend. But this Gallegos guy, he was like your archenemy right?"

"Well, not quite."

"Yeah, but he'd be as interested in hurting you as in dating her, right? Logical for him to go after her, then."

"She could have waited a little longer."

"Well, some girls are more interested in being with someone than in who they're with. You'd already been gone almost a week. She wouldn't want to miss out on any dances or anything."

"You're a cold-hearted . . ."

Dad pushed the door open and stuck his head in. Dave-Dad. "Will?"

"Yeah?"

He came in, giving Cecilia a look. She winked at me, bounced up off the bed, and left. Dad came into the room as she went out.

"Are you coming down?" he asked.

"I don't know," I said.

"Why not?"

Good question. "I just feel..."

"Yes?"

"They're strangers! I don't know any of those people down there. I don't feel like I... belong there."

"They're the same people you wanted to see when you got home a month ago."

"Don't you ever get sick of being right about everything?"

"I'm not right about quite everything, so no. I feel pretty good when I am." He came across the room and sat on the edge of the bed. "They're not really strangers. They're your family. They all love you and care about you, and they're here because they want to let you know that. This is the first time I've let the relatives visit since you got here, and every one of them showed up."

"Not every one," I said.

"Who's missing?"

I didn't answer him directly. I looked down at the

pencil I was holding and said, "In two years I'll be eighteen. I can do whatever I want, then. Live where I want."

"Oh, I know that. Cecilia's already planning to go to an out-of-state college just to get away faster. I'm hoping though that by then you'll understand how much a part of this family you really are and always have been and how much you mean to us all."

"So I'll stay here?"

"No. So you'll make your choices based on something other than anger."

Bingo, I thought. I did want to go back to New Mexico to see Dad (Bill-Dad) and my friends and all. But he was right about that anger business, too. Sometimes I still thought about leaving here just to get back at him for bringing me the way he did. But leaving here was no answer to anything either. Now that I had them back again, losing Mom and Cecilia and Dad (Dave-Dad) would hurt too much. "I'm not really all that mad anymore," I said. "Most of the time."

"But?"

"But... If I'm really so much a part of this family, why was I named after him?"

"Him who? Mr. Melendez?" He sounded surprised. "You weren't named after him. Whatever gave you that idea?"

"We have the same name."

"I thought he had some strange-sounding Spanish name. Gilberto or something."

"Guillermo. Guillermo Santiago. Guillermo is Spanish for William, and Santiago is a nickname for St. James. Guillermo Santiago translates roughly to William James."

Dave threw back his head and laughed.

"You've heard me call him Bill before," I said. It didn't seem so funny to me.

"I thought 'Bill' was just some rodeo nickname he used!" Dave said. "Well, I guess these things can happen, they're common enough names. Son, you were named after your two grandfathers: William Trevor and James Campbell, who are both, incidentally, downstairs waiting to see you. Along with a lot of other people. What say we give it a try?"

"If anyone says anything stupid, like 'How does it feel to be kidnapped,' I'm gonna deck them."

"Keep in mind that those people waiting down there are nervous, just like you are. Happy, excited, and anxious, but nervous too. Nervous people sometimes say stupid things without meaning to. And believe me, if anyone does say anything stupid, he'll feel plenty bad enough without you decking him."

I felt myself smiling, even though I hadn't meant to.

Dad smiled back and stood up. "Shall we go?"

"Yeah. I guess so." I put down the pencil and got up, and Dad put his hand out to pat my shoulder as we headed for the door. It opened as I got there, though. Mom came in.

"There you are, honey. Got your homework done yet?"

She hugged me. It was just a quick squeeze that she meant to give, a friendly hello hug like she'd been passing out to relatives all morning. But I caught her in both arms and gave her a real hug, the kind of long, long hug I should have given her a month ago when I first saw her again. I had held her then, while she cried, but I hadn't hugged her. I hugged her now, and had the sudden, stupid desire to be ten years old again, and small enough for her to wrap me up in her arms completely, like she used to.

"Honey, are you all right?" Mom said.

"I'm fine, Mom," I said. "I'm fine." But my voice cracked. I couldn't help it. I had started crying, hugging her, and I couldn't stop.

"Will! What is it?"

"Nothing, really. I'm sorry, I just..."

I felt Dad's hand on my shoulder again and turned, embarrassed at the tears streaking down my face. It was so stupid! He didn't say anything though. He just wrapped his arms around me, like he had in the police station in Santa Fe. Only this time, I hugged him back.

"Dave, something's wrong!" Mom said. "Will's crying!"

"Maybe it's about time he did," Dave said.